MARY-MARGARET
and the CASE of the
lapsed
parishioner

MARY-MARGARET
and the CASE of the
lapsed
parishioner

A Pint of Trouble Mystery

DESMOND P. RYAN

LEVEL
BEST BOOKS

First published by Level Best Books 2023

First edition

ISBN: 978-1-68512-438-0

Cover art by Level Best Designs

This book was professionally typeset on Reedsy.
Find out more at reedsy.com

To Daisy Ryan

Praise for Mary-Margaret and the Case of the Lapsed Parishioner

"Mary-Margaret and the Case of the Lapsed Parishioner stands out among cozies because it is so easy to identify with the main character, Mary-Margaret O'Shea who is Everygrandma. No matter your nationality, religion, race, or gender, you likely have or had a Mary-Margaret in your life. She's a warm, feisty, irreverent (but always in a classy way), damn-the-torpedoes, no-holds-barred kind of amateur sleuth. Surrounded by characters both off the wall (especially Arthur, her they/them sidekick) and rational (her often-beleaguered police office son Mike, and her friends from the Old Country, Eleanor and Angus Corrigan), Mary-Margaret uses perception, instinct, and sometimes bald-faced lies to solve the murder of a parishioner of her church."—Cheryl Freedman, freelance editor, retired executive director of Crime Writers of Canada

"Mary-Margaret is irreverent, hysterical, and smart as a whip. The story drew me in and I didn't want it to end. Can't wait for the next one!"—Lynn McPherson, author of The Izzy Walsh Mystery Series

"Don't let her size fool you—Mary-Margaret O'Shea rules! The book had me laughing the entire time I was reading. Can't wait for the next one in this fabulous new series!"—Dark & Stormy Book Club

Chapter One

Mary-Margaret O'Shea looked at her watch for the fifth time in twelve minutes, then shook it vigorously just in case it wasn't working properly. It was, and still no sign of Jane Ann Hill, one of the parishioners, albeit somewhat lapsed, at St. Francis of Assisi who had volunteered to help this morning.

Not the day for a lie-in, me girl, Mary-Margaret thought. We've more clothing than a doxies got dates that need sortin' and I canna do it meself.

She pulled out her cell phone and called the number she had for Jane Ann and left yet another message; it joined the nine she had already left.

Ach, what if somethin' has come of the lamb? And here am I, worryin' about a wee bit of sortin'. Best to get on with it and hope she shows up.

Although she had retired as church secretary a few months ago, Mary-Margaret found herself back now at St. Francis of Assisi to manage the fall bazaar. It should have been the responsibility of Ashleigh, The New Girl. The New Girl, however, was floating around in the Caribbean at the moment on her honeymoon. Had the proceeds of this event not funded the daily breakfast programs for three daycares within the parish, the planning of the bazaar would not have been of such importance, and The New Girl's absence would have been a non-issue. As things stood, however, Father Miguel had no choice but to ask Mary-Margaret to come back for a couple of weeks to ensure that the bazaar took place and was the success it had been in previous years.

Being the good soldier, Mary-Margaret had agreed to return, only to regret her decision almost the moment she set foot back in her former

1

office. Amongst other things, she discovered that her successor had failed to organize the volunteers to help prepare for the big day, nor had any local businesses been contacted to donate raffle prizes. Simply put, things were a mess. Having raised four children mostly on her own, however, she had developed a knack for sorting out messes. As such, Mary-Margaret called in a few favors and the regulars sent in their donations for the raffle. The hardest part of her job was to get at least one person a day to come in to help sort the bags of used clothing the parishioners had dropped off over the past few weeks. But she did it.

Today was Jane Ann Hill's day, and she was not here. After a morning spent checking her watch, calling Jane Ann several more times, and then sorting through bags of sweaters, pants, and mismatched socks on her own, Mary-Margaret was ready for a break.

Nothin' to do for it but to put on a kettle, she thought, making her way from the cluttered parlor towards what used to be her office.

"Everything all right?" Father Miguel asked as he walked past her in the hallway.

"Everythin's fine, Father," Mary-Margaret replied, not missing a step and knowing full well that he must have passed by the room several times during the morning and seen her sorting the clothes alone. If only Father Brian was still here. He'd be in there like a dirty shirt, helping.

"Considerin' that I'm on me own with a room full of things needin' to be sorted by Friday," she added.

Remembering how disproportionately dependent the smooth running of his days had rested on the ups and downs of Mary-Margaret's own day, Father Miguel knew that it was in his best interest to try to help her deal with her problem.

"Where are your volunteers?" he asked, following her to the front office.

"Volunteer," Mary-Margaret corrected, plugging in the kettle she had brought from her son's house, where she had been staying the last couple of weeks.

"Where's the Keurig? It makes tea as well, you know." Father Miguel looked around for the new coffeemaker Ashleigh had set up.

"Away. Ye canna make a good cuppa in under five minutes. Regardless," Mary-Margaret continued, reaching into the desk drawer to pull out a Barry's tea bag she had also brought from Michael's house. "The New Girl seems to have neglected to sign up any volunteers, so I've been left to me own devices to rally the troops. Luckily, Jane Ann Hill, who was a part of the congregation many years ago, agreed to help. Said she was available for this mornin', she did, and now she's not shown up."

"Did you give her a call?"

"Many times. Ye may think I do nothin' but sit on me backside and sip tea all day, Father, but even now, comin' in from me retirement—at yer request as ye may recall—I am the one who runs this church day-to-day."

Father Miguel bit his lip, annoyed at himself for having called in the woman who had been left as a legacy from previous priests after finally having gotten rid of her.

"Still biting yer lip, Father? Clearly nerves. Ye know, Father Brian had such horrible stage fright before every Mass—"

"It is not nerves that causes me to bite my lip, Mary-Margaret. Now, what happened when you called your volunteer?"

"No answer. On any of the calls I made to her. Now if ye don't mind, I've got a kettle waitin' for me, unless ye would like to join me for a cuppa?"

"Perhaps another time. I've got some paperwork to do." Father Miguel was turning to leave when he noticed a pair of crutches leaning against the wall in the corner. "What are those for?"

"Well, Father," Mary-Margaret sighed, "it's a long story."

"Oh, God."

"But I'll cut to the chase. As ye will recall, just after I retired, me Michael, the Big City Police Detective, got beaten to near death while arrestin' that murderer. Was in all the papers. I, of course, immediately packed up me things and went to look after him. Time passes, and he's thinkin' he's better, but I can see that he's still a pint below the quart. That's both the gift and the curse of motherhood, Father: knowin' what yer children need. Anyway, I was just out with Sally-next-door's dog thinkin' about how to bring me Michael 'round to the notion that I ought to stay on when the wee pup

3

knocks into me. Of course, I'm fine, but some eejit at the dog park called an ambulance."

"I see," Father Miguel said, holding his hand to his mouth to stop biting his lip.

"Because of me age, the paramedics thought I ought to go to the hospital. Of course, me foot was fine, but this is where it came to me, Father: if me foot was broken, there would be no way me Michael would send me home."

"So you lied and told your son your foot was broken?"

"Well, yes, but the end justifies the means, so while I did lie, when all is said and done, no one will mind. Borrowed a pair of crutches that I saw by the nurses' station on me way out and have been hobblin' around on them, more or less, ever since."

"So you lied and stole?"

"Fibbed and will return the crutches in another few weeks, yes."

"Do you not think anyone has noticed that you don't have a cast on your foot?"

"Well, here's the thing of it, Father. I said I was part of a test group."

"A test group?"

"That's me story, yes. And this is how it goes: the hospital is working on this castless method wherein they..."

Not waiting to hear the rest, Father Miguel walked out of the office shaking his head as he made his way down the hall towards his own office, silently cursing himself for even remotely having imagined that bringing Mary-Margaret back, even for a couple of weeks, was a good idea.

Mary-Margaret, meanwhile, turned her attention to the boiling kettle, thankful that she didn't have to explain herself to this young priest any further.

She heard a slight cough a few feet away from her.

"Jesus, Mary, and Joseph. Could ye not have knocked, me girl?" she yelped, almost scalding herself with the boiling water she was pouring, in the absence of a teapot, into her mug.

"Sorry. Are you Mary-Margaret?" the woman asked.

"I am."

"And are you doing the sorting for the bazaar on Saturday?"

"Apparently I am, yes."

"I'm Chrystal Hill. I was just down the hall looking for my mother, Jane Ann Hill."

"Pleased to meet ye, I'm sure. And I have been lookin' for yer mam all mornin' meself."

"I was supposed to pick her up here and then take her for lunch."

"Well, she's not here. I'm just makin' meself a cuppa. Hopefully, she's just runnin' late. Would ye care for one whilst ye wait?"

Mary-Margaret looked around for a second mug. Finding none, she decided again: *The New Girl clearly has a lot to learn about bein' a church secretary.*

"She's not here?"

"No. And here I've been, on me own, sortin' away for the past two hours."

"That's unlike her. From what I know of her, she's punctual to a fault."

"Well, I can't vouch for that, but I'm assumin' that when yer mam says she's goin' to be somewhere, there she be."

"Do you think something has happened to her?"

"I don't know, luv. I gave her at least a dozen rings, I'd have to say. The first six or so were between nine and nine-thirty and then it just became more of a habit, and I carried on until about ten-thirty, and there was never an answer. Have ye given her a ring?"

"No. I assumed she'd be here. I'll give her a call now."

I canna possibly have a cuppa on me own, but I'll drop without one.

"No answer," Chrystal said.

"Well, maybe she's stuck in transit. Ye know, this city isn't gettin' any easier to run around in."

"She lives in the co-op around the corner. She would have walked here."

"Since when? I thought she'd moved into one of those luxury condos downtown, which is why she stopped comin' to church. That and Father Brian leavin', of course," Mary-Margaret said, pulling the teabag from her mug.

"She did move. And now she's back. It's a long story."

5

"Well, I'm sure we've all got a long story or two hidden in our pantries."

"You're right about that," Chrystal said with a sad smile. "But I am wondering where she is now."

"Me son is a police detective. Do ye want me to give him a ring, then?"

"No, I'm sure it's nothing serious." It was obvious to Mary-Margaret that Chrystal was trying to convince herself more than anyone else.

"Suit yerself, luv, but me son tells me about his investigations all the time. Says most people report their loved ones missin' far too late for the police to do anythin'. Says someone is missin' as soon as they're out of their routine and not where they're supposed to be. Might that sound like yer mam now?"

She passed the mug of tea to Chrystal, deciding that the younger woman needed it far more than she did.

"Ach, look at ye. Yer hands are shakin' like the legs of a newborn lamb. Why don't ye give the police a call. Maybe she's been in an accident."

Chrystal's knees buckled under her. Mary-Margaret grabbed the mug and helped the younger woman to a chair before she could fall to the ground.

"I'm not sayin' she has, luv, but it would rule things out if ye called, don't ye think? Here, use the phone on me desk in front of ye. I'll just step out for a moment to give ye some privacy."

With that, Mary-Margaret walked down the hall to Father Miguel's office.

"So I see your volunteer has arrived," he said with some satisfaction.

"No, that would be her daughter. Jane Ann's missin'."

"Missing? Always one for the dramatic, aren't we?"

"Drama or no, the woman's not here, she's not answerin' her phone, and her daughter has no idea where she is, so I'd say she's missin'."

"I'm sure she'll turn up." That said, Father Miguel looked back at his computer screen.

"Father," Mary-Margaret said, sitting down in the chair on the other side of his desk, "do ye think ye could perhaps tear yerself away from yer work here and offer a word of comfort to the girl?"

"Comfort?"

"Yes. Ye know—reassurance? Support? Hope?"

"I know what comfort means, Mary-Margaret," the young priest said, straightening up in his chair.

"Sometimes I wonder," Mary-Margaret muttered under her breath.

"I understand that there is a room full of clothing that has to be sorted and priced by—when was it? Friday?"

"I hear God's work summonsin' me, Father," Mary-Margaret said tartly as she got up and left the room.

"At least you take direction from someone," the priest mumbled.

"I heard that!"

* * *

"Well, me luv?" Mary-Margaret asked, reentering her old office just as Chrystal was hanging up the phone.

"They say she hasn't been taken to any of the hospitals."

"That's a good sign."

"But I don't think it's like her to not answer her phone, especially if she's late."

"That's not a good sign."

"No. So I've reported her missing."

"I'm sure she'll turn up, safe and sound, sooner than later. In the meantime, if I may ask, would ye mind helpin' me get ready for the bazaar? I could use another set of hands, and it might help take yer mind off of this until she turns up."

Chapter Two

"Detective O'Shea. How may I help you?" a gruff voice said.

"Michael, this is yer mother callin'."

"Mom?" His voice softened.

"The very same. Listen, me son, I need yer help." Mary-Margaret said, holding the phone close to her face.

"Are you okay?"

"Of course, I'm okay. It's not me I'm callin' about. It's about one of our parishioners...lapsed parishioners, if the truth need be tellin'. She's missin'."

"Hold on a minute."

"Don't worry, lad. She's already been reported. I'm just wonderin' what's been done about it so far."

"When was she reported missing?"

"About an hour ago."

"Then I'd say nothing has been done," Michael said with a sigh.

"Nothin'?" Mary-Margaret said, pulling the phone away from her ear to give it a closer look before putting it back.

"Nothing."

"And we pay yer salaries then, do we?"

"Don't start, Mom."

"A woman has been reported missin' and ye have done not a thing about it. She could be this minute bein' beaten by some sadist or sexually molested by—"

"Doubtful. What is her name?"

"Jane Ann Hill. Have ye got her on yer computer, then?"

"Just give me a minute." There was a pause. "Yes. Okay. Says she was reported missing by her daughter about an hour ago."

"Yes, I know that," Mary-Margaret exclaimed. "That's what I was just tellin' ye."

"No addiction, no mental health issues, no—wait a minute, why am I telling you this?"

"Because I'm yer mother. Now, where are yer lads lookin' for her?"

"They're not."

"What? That makes no sense to me at all, me son."

"She's not considered a high risk for—"

"For what? Murder? Well then, what if the poor woman has got amnesia and is wandering about in the woods somewhere?"

"What woods, Mom? We live in the city," Michael said patiently.

"I dunno, me son. Some woods. There are parkland and ravines and the like, ye know. Or worse yet, maybe she's fallen into the lake and is this very moment flailin' madly."

"Unlikely."

"Ach, I dunno why I even called."

"I love you, too, Mom."

"There has not been a moment since before ye were born that I have not loved ye, Michael, but there have been many moments since that have tried me patience. So what ye are telling me is that there's nothin' ye can do."

"Not right now, Mom. No."

"Well, I'll not keep ye from yer real police work then. Bye-bye bye bye-bye."

* * *

"Dare I ask?" Father Miguel said, poking his head in Mary-Margaret's office.

"One of yer flock is missing, Father, and the police are doin' not a thing about it."

"I take it that this is about the woman from this morning?"

"The very same, Father."

"No signs of foul play?"

"I have no idea, Father. I've just this moment gotten off the phone with me Michael, who was as useless as a pair of ice skates at a swimmin' pool."

"I see. Well, I'm sure that if there was anything—"

"No disrespect intended, Father, and I hate to cut ye short, but once I've had me tea, I'll be busier than a one-armed paper hanger gettin' things ready for the bazaar, so unless ye have any words to offer...?"

"No, I'm done. Enjoy your tea, Mary-Margaret."

* * *

Mary-Margaret got on the bus to make her way home, but, unlike this morning, it was well past rush hour, and the bus was practically empty. She carefully settled herself down in her preferred seat at the front of the bus, adjacent to the driver. She missed the days before the plexiglass dividers separated the drivers from everyone else when she would talk to the driver about everything from the weather to world politics. These days, she usually brought something to read to pass the time instead.

After opening her book, Mary-Margaret found her mind wandering to the events of the day and, for no particular reason except that he was the only other occupant, her eyes settled on the young man at the back of the bus.

Seeing that the young man was looking back at her, Mary-Margaret looked down at her book and pretended to read for the remainder of her ride, but not before noticing that he had a cloth sack that looked like a pillowcase bulging on either sides, full of items that were unlikely pillows.

Chapter Three

I t was early evening before Mary-Margaret got back to Michael's house and had a moment to put her feet up to enjoy a cuppa. She was just settling in when there was a knock at the door.

"Ach, it never ends!" she muttered before grabbing the crutches she had placed beside her and making her way to the front door. She took a look through the tiny glass panel at the top and saw Frank Maloney standing on the doorstep.

"Come in, yer out," she said as she opened the door.

"Mary-Margaret, what's happened?" Frank asked as he stepped inside, giving her a quick hug while she set the crutches against the wall by the door. He was a wiry man just past sixty who, like Mary-Margaret, had left Ireland almost half a century before. Like Mary-Margaret, he sounded as if he'd just left the Emerald Isle that morning.

"'Tis a long story for another day. Shorthand: Me foot is fine. But I've had just such a day, Francis." She led him into the sparsely furnished living room, motioning him to sit.

"Fair ball." He knew better than to ask questions. They had met at O'Leary's Pub more than twenty years ago when Mary-Margaret and her son were having dinner. Frank suspected that she wouldn't have given him a second glance if Michael hadn't recognized him as one of the attendants from the morgue and introduced them.

"Is everythin' all right then, luv?" he asked with more tenderness than, in Mary-Margaret's opinion, was necessary. In fact, had she been more rested, she would have been annoyed. Over the course of their friendship, which she was sure Frank had fostered by continuing to appear at her local every week after that one evening, she had given no indication whatsoever that she had any romantic interest in him at all. He was a good man, but he was no Jimmy, her long-deceased husband that she has mourned every day since his passing. Still, she didn't want to hurt Frank's feelings. And it was always good to have a man about.

"I'm barely hangin' on by the tips of me fingers at the moment, truth to be told. I'm sure I'll feel better once I've had a wee sit and a sip of me tea. Would ye like a cuppa? Help yerself if ye would. Mugs are just in the cupboard beside the fridge there in the kitchen. I'm too tired to make me way over to pour it for ye."

"Of course, Mary-Margaret. Sit, and I'll be right back."

He called from the kitchen, "Have ye got any of those wee biscuits here?"

"They'd be in the bottom cupboard by the sink if there are any. Our Max is very fond of them. And tell me yer not wearin' yer shoes in the house? Last time ye were at me own house with them on, Sally-next-door's dog almost had a seizure with all the sniffin' he did."

"Sorry about that, luv. Must have forgotten to change them before leavin' work. Regardless, I've got me clean ones on now, and I'll kick them off when I bring in me tea." Frank poured himself a cup and brought a plate of biscuits into the living room for the two of them to share.

"No harm, no foul, I suppose. Although the thought of bodily fluids on me floors does make me stomach turn a wee bit. Didn't bother to tell Arthur about it. Poor soul would have likely up and quit, and then who'd clean me house? Not that Arthur's much of a house cleaner at the best of times."

"Here, have a biscuit. That'll bring ye round." Frank sat down beside Mary-Margaret and offered her the plate.

"Ta. Nothing like a wee biscuit and a good cuppa to bring ye back to yerself," she agreed, savoring both.

"Unless it's a dram of Jameson!" Frank said with a wink of his eye.

"Ha! I think just the smell of that would put me under this evening, although I'm sure Michael's got a bottle of it if ye are interested."

Before Frank could answer, a small Jack Russell terrier came bounding

12

down the stairs and leapt onto his lap.

"Off, Phil," Mary-Margaret ordered. "Ye know better, pup."

"Ye have got Sally-next-door's dog with ye, then?" Frank said, steadying the contents of his mug as the dog bounded off his lap with the same enthusiasm that had landed him there.

"Ach, poor wee thing. Still needs walking, broken foot or not."

"But I thought you said yer foot was fine."

"A good liar I am not," she said with a laugh. "To keep the story straight in me mind, I just tell meself that when I'm here, me foot is broken. When I'm away, it's not. Otherwise, I'd not know whether I was comin' or goin'."

"So why is Phil here if ye are sayin' ye have a broken foot and ye are here?"

"Well, luv, this is where it gets complicated. I told Michael it was easier for me to have Phil here full-time, and Sally-next-door was fine with it. I also told Michael that there are enough dog-walkers in this neighborhood for me to hire one to walk Phil and that I would be chargin' it to Sally-next-door."

"That makes no sense, luv."

"Well, here's the truth of the matter, then. I think Max needs a dog. Every lad should have a dog, but Michael is dead set against it."

"Did Michael have a dog when he was a lad, then?"

"No. But we are talkin' about me grandson now. As I was sayin', Max needs a dog and Phil needs company. I'm thinkin' with Phil here, Michael will warm up to the idea, and then... Ach, the logic behind it is too complicated for me mind to unravel to ye in this moment."

"It was that kind of day, was it, luv?"

"'Twas. First and always, dealin' with Father Miguel. It never gets easier, ye know."

"Why did ye offer to go back, then? Ye dunna need the agro."

"He needs me. And then me car is at me house because I told Michael I broke me right foot and can't drive, so I need something to do to keep me busy durin' the day. And it will only be for another week."

"I still dunna think this lyin' to yer Michael is a good idea, Mary-Margaret. And I dunna believe for a moment that he's buyin' this bill o' goods ye are sellin'. Nor do I believe ye believe he believes ye. All of this muckin' about has got to be weighin' heavy on ye, no?"

"Well, 'tis. But that's not what's fillin' me mind at the moment. One of our parishioners who was me volunteer—me only volunteer for today—was reported missin' to the police."

"What does yer Michael have to say about it?"

"Ach, he was too busy doing *real* police work to be of any assistance."

"I find that hard to believe, Mary-Margaret," Frank suggested gently. "Maybe there just wasn't anythin' to report?"

"Whose side are ye on?" Mary-Margaret said with a smile, playfully swatting at Frank.

"I'm just sayin'. Maybe there's nothin' to it. Maybe she just had a change of heart, wanted to get away for a wee bit, didn't tell anyone. Sortin' through other peoples' clothin' isn't everyone's idea of fun, even if it is fer the church and all."

"Well, I can tell ye that it's not my idea of a day by the Irish Sea either, but her daughter came by to pick her up and was quite concerned, which leads me to believe that there may be somethin' to it."

"That does put a nail in it, then. Won't be the first missing person to end up on me mortuary trolley."

"Hardly upliftin', Francis."

"Sorry, luv. Sometimes I forget that I'm not at work when I'm talking to ye."

"It's me son who is the policeman, not me." Mary-Margaret said with a laugh.

"Well, he must get his smarts from somewhere."

"Must be from his Da, God rest his soul."

"God rest his soul," Frank echoed.

Both of them sipped at their tea.

"So what are ye goin' to do about yer missin' lady?"

"What can I do?"

"Why not give yer Michael another ring? See if there are any updates?"

"Ach, I think I'll leave it. And besides, he's home here upstairs sleepin' now. At least, I hope he is. Lad works day and night, does me Michael."

"Why not talk to him about it in the mornin', then? In the meantime," Frank said, finishing his tea, "I think it would be best for ye if I took me leave and called it a night. Unless ye want me to stay?"

"No, I think ye are wise. And thank ye for stoppin' by. I'll be better company tomorrow night, I'm thinkin'."

"Let's hope so."

"And what do ye mean by that, Francis Maloney?" Mary-Margaret said, tilting her head to one side as she crossed her arms.

"Have a good rest, me luv, and we'll see ye tomorrow then. Dunna worry. I'll let meself out."

Frank took his empty mug to the kitchen, then returning to the living room, gave Mary-Margaret a soft kiss on her forehead, and left.

"Safe home, lad," Mary-Margaret called out after him.

Then she took her mug to the kitchen before remembering that she had left her crutches by the front door.

Thank God me Michael is asleep and didn't see that. I canna keep this up forever, though. I told him six weeks and then rehab. We'll not have to sort anything until after that. Time to get up to bed and do some readin' to take me mind off it all.

Picking up her crutches by the front door, she hobbled to the bottom of the stairs and attempted to take a step up. Then she stopped.

Ach, I could break both me legs tryin' to get up the stairs if I was to use these things!

She picked up the crutches and carried them up the stairs with her, hastily turning off the lights immediately after reaching the second floor just in case anyone was there to see her.

Chapter Four

"You're up early," Michael said as he walked into the kitchen.

"The same could be said of ye, lad." Mary-Margaret, startled at his sudden appearance, grabbed the crutches she had brought downstairs with her and pulled them under her arms. *Thanks be to God I remembered to bring these blessed things with me. Canna be too careful in this house.* "And don't ye look smart. Goin' to Mass the mornin', are we?"

"Court."

"Ach, I don't know how ye do it, workin' night and day. No mind. I'll get some rollies on for ye, then."

"Should you be on your feet, Mom?" he asked, reaching around her to turn on the coffee maker.

"Me? It would take more than a broken ankle—"

"I thought it was your foot." Michael took a closer look at his mother. "But I guess it's hard to tell without a cast."

"Foot. Yes, that's what I meant. Same thing. And it would be a frosty day in Dublin before yer mother would be lettin' somethin' like a broken limb on any part of her body stop her from lookin' after her family. Now reach up and get me that big pot for the rolled oats. I was just lookin' out the back door here and seein' that it's a gorgeous mornin'—"

"Mom, we've been over this. I don't eat breakfast."

"Therein lies yer problem, luv. Grab me that pot, and I'll have a bowl ready for ye in twenty minutes."

"Hi, Gran," Max said, wiping the sleep from his eyes as he wandered into the room. "Did you make enough coffee for me, Dad?"

16

"Sorry, no. I didn't think you'd be up."

"Good mornin', me lamb. I've got some of those pastries ye love in the fridge. Let me just pop them in the oven to warm them now. And I'll get a cuppa for ye."

"How come he doesn't need to eat rolled oats?" Michael complained.

"He's young. His constitution doesn't need all of that fiber. Ye don't want to be gettin' yerself bunged up at yer age, Michael, trust me. Now have a glass of water to start. All of that coffee can't be good for ye. Max, here's yer cuppa, luv. Three sugars, isn't it?"

Michael reached past his mother to retrieve a travel mug from the cupboard, then poured coffee into it and walked towards the front door.

* * *

Carryin' these ruddy crutches 'round will be the death of me yet, Mary-Margaret thought, hoisting them up the steps of the bus. She juggled them under one arm while rooting in her purse for her pass, still managing to grab at the pole just in time to steady herself as the bus started off again. After giving the driver a look with the intent just shy of killing him, given that he was driving the bus, her spirits sank even lower as she scanned the hopelessly packed vehicle for a seat.

Then, a man a few seats down from where she was standing, stood up. She nodded appreciatively at him and the people around her who had shuffled themselves enough for her to get to that seat. A woman helped her sit down, holding the crutches for her until she could get herself settled. Ah well, Mary-Margaret thought, the crutches do come in handy upon occasion.

Looking out the window, she noticed the neighborhoods changing as they got closer to the church. Large houses with tiny, immaculate gardens gave way to large houses with overrun front gardens that, in turn, gave way to rundown houses with no gardens. The upscale specialty shops became bargain stores became empty storefronts. Even the cars parked on the street seemed to depreciate in value as they got closer to St. Francis of Assisi Catholic Church.

The bus emptied more and more with each stop, until only Mary-Margaret and a couple of scruffy-looking young men at the back. One of them looked like the guy from the night before, *sans* pillowcase and its contents. The more she stared, the more she decided that they were likely homeless and looking for a way to pass the time. When she reached her stop, she pulled the cord that activated the bell. The driver stopped, and she stepped off, carrying her crutches.

Once at the church, Mary-Margaret decided that she would try giving Jane Ann Hill a call right after she had made herself a cuppa. Flipping the kettle on, she dialed the number.

No answer.

We'll not sort anythin' this way. Frank was likely right: me Michael will have come 'round by now.

She dialed her son's cell number.

Straight to voicemail.

"Good morning, Mary-Margaret. Have you got your volunteers lined up for today?"

"Oh, Father, ye startled me."

"Nerves, is it? You know, if coming back like this is too much—"

"Absolutely not, Father. Ye called me back, and I am here for the duration."

"Oh."

"Now if ye have nothin' more to ask of me...?"

"No, I was just passing by."

"Very kind of ye, Father. Now, if ye'll excuse me while I settle me nerves with a cuppa..."

Father Miguel turned and walked down the hall, wondering what lesson God had intended him to learn by placing Mary-Margaret back in his church.

* * *

Mary-Margaret never thought the day would come when she would be glad to see Laura-Jean McQueen, but today was that day. While there was nothing particularly wrong with Laura-Jean McQueen, Mary-Margaret had to go a full country mile to find anything particularly right about her. Nonetheless, she was here, as promised, to sort for the bazaar.

"Since ye have got the hang of it, I've got some work for Father Miguel to attend to," she announced within minutes of the two women settling in the parlor.

"No, you don't. Ashleigh told me you were brought back just to handle the bazaar."

"Be that as it may, Laura-Jean, but The New Girl doesn't quite have a grasp on all that needs doin' here at the church, and as everyone knows, I do, and I intend on gettin' it done now. So will you be needin' anythin' before I go, or are ye all right?"

"I'll be fine, thank you."

Mary-Margaret stomped into her office, threw herself into her chair, and slammed her hands down on the computer keyboard, causing the screen to come to life.

Ach, as if I need that one tellin' me how to do me job. As if I don't know every inch of this parish and all of the secrets it holds. As if... Oh, for the love of all that is sacred, don't tell me The New Girl has changed all of me passwords!

She hammered in a few more iterations of the numbers and letters of passwords she recalled, finally unlocking the file that contained the addresses of all of the parishioners. She quickly scrolled down the list until she came to Jane Ann's address. It was one that Mary-Margaret recognized and was not within this parish.

Recalling that Chrystal had said that her mother had moved from the posh condo into a co-op near the church, Mary-Margaret clicked on Google Maps and did a virtual walk through the neighborhood.

Ach, this must be it. The name's written right across the front of it, and it's just 'round the corner here. If me Michael isn't going to help, perhaps I'll just waltz meself over and give a wee knock at the door.

She looked over at the crutches in the corner. *Ye can wait here until days' end. Pointless wastin' me best hobblin' when there's no one needin' to notice noticin'.*

Chapter Five

The walk did Mary-Margaret a world of good. The crisp air had that smell of autumn that reminded her that winter wasn't far off. She'd have to get her car into the mechanic's to have the snow tires put on sooner rather than later, but how to do it this year? She couldn't drive the car herself if she was telling Michael that her right foot was broken and Max didn't have his full license yet. Perhaps Frank would take the car in, but she didn't want to ask just in case he got the wrong idea about how things stood in their friendship.

Arthur would do it. *A good lad, is that one.*

With that conundrum solved, she set her mind to Jane Ann and what she knew about this woman, which was precious little.

Why am I burstin' me bustle to find her then? She's got family. A daughter, anyway. Although her understandin' of her own mam seemed a bit dodgy to me. Regardless, no one but me and the girl seem terribly concerned for her, so why am I...?

She stopped and looked around her, noticing that she was no longer in the nicest part—if there was such a place—of this rough neighborhood. Not that the difference between nice and not-so-nice was completely noticeable. Not like Sibby Mac's neighborhood.

Ach, what if this is another Sibby Mac? she thought, recalling her son's most recent homicide investigation. *What if our Jane Ann has just lately been involved with some fancy fella just like our Sibby Mac was? And what if she's gone off and got herself murdered and stuffed in a steamer trunk as well? Or what if she's bein' held hostage by some hooligans? Ach no, I can't walk away from this. If me Michael thinks me daft, then I'll* just *remind him of how I gave him a clue or two to pass along that helped find our Sibby Mac's killer, I will.*

She looked at the numbers on the buildings to her right, picking up her pace until she came to a low-rise where, as clear as in the picture on her computer, she saw the words *Craig Stillwell Co-Op* chiseled into a huge—and unnatural-looking—rock that sat in front of the building where a garden might have been.

In fact, as soon as I get meself back to the church, I'll be ringin' Michael and get him on board. I'll be needin' a good lunch, and he'll probably take a pint if I'm offerin' to foot the bill.

* * *

Judging by the age of the apartment building and the look of the lock on the front door, Mary-Margaret figured giving the handle a quick pull might work just as well as having an actual key.

Just as she was about to give the door a tug, it flew open, and a middle-aged man whose salt and pepper hair was cut in a manner that reminded Mary-Margaret of the ill-conceived bowl cuts she used to give the boys when they were young pushed past her, almost knocking her down. Before she could decide which piece of her mind she would give him, he had hightailed it down the street, his shirttails flapping behind him. Rather than make any effort to pursue him to scold him for his rudeness—not that making such an effort would be at all effective—and not wishing to test her theory about the feebleness of the lock, Mary-Margaret grabbed the door before it slammed shut.

Once inside the building, Mary-Margaret checked the listings on the wall and found a J. Hill with an apartment number beside it. She walked up the five steps to the first-floor apartments and found what she assumed would be Jane Ann's door, annoyed that The New Girl hadn't updated any of the files since taking over what Mary-Margaret had built into quite an empire of information. That Jane Ann might not have provided updated information seemed to slip Mary-Margaret's mind in the moment. It did, however, cross her mind that 'J. Hill' could be just about anyone.

She took a deep breath and was just about to knock on the door when she stopped.

And what shall I be sayin' when she answers the door? 'Missed ye at the sortin'?' 'Chose this day to give up answerin' yer cell?' 'Glad ye aren't dead?' And what if it isn't her?

"Looking for someone?" a woman called from down the corridor.

Think. Think fast.

"Me...sister, Jane Ann. Do ye know her?"

"Sister, eh? I didn't know she had a sister. You do kind of look alike, though," the woman commented as she drew nearer.

"She's the prettier one," Mary-Margaret said, expecting the woman to contradict her. When she did not, Mary-Margaret considered that slap in the face was not in vain. At least she knew she had the right address.

"She certainly can put it on when she wants to, can't she?"

"That she can," Mary-Margaret said with a sigh, and then added, "She's always been like that. Very popular with the lads back in the day."

"I don't doubt that for a second. I've only been here a couple of months and have made it my business to get to know everyone, and a woman her age with a boyfriend the age of Jerry—"

"Grand. Listen, me sister is expectin' me. I've just now landed from overseas—Ireland, where I live—which is why..."

The woman looked at the floor around Mary-Margaret.

"Ach, me luggage. The airline lost it. That's what ye get fer flyin' anythin' but Aer Lingus. I told Jane Ann—she's the one who booked me tickets, don't ye know—not to bother signin' me up for any of those foreign airlines, but—"

"Don't overseas flights usually arrive at night?" the woman asked, taking a closer look at Mary-Margaret.

"Yes. Exactly, they do, but the flight was delayed and came in very, very late, and me, with me lost luggage, was at the airport until just a few hours ago, when I hopped on yer transit and made me way here. It's not been an easy go."

The two women looked at each other, neither one moving.

"Ach, where are me manners, then? Me name is Mary-Margaret," she said, holding out her hand.

"Nancy," the younger woman finally said with a firmer grip than Mary-Margaret anticipated, given the size of the woman. "My name is Nancy. I'm the superintendent."

"Glad to meet ye," Mary-Margaret said. "Absolutely flah'ed out, I am. Could murder a cuppa, truth to be told. And, oh! I called me sister, usin' a payphone at the airport o' course, to pick me up there when we landed in the wee hours of the mornin'. With all of this upset, I forgot all about callin' her with an update, and here I am. She's probably there waitin' for me now. And me keys to the apartment, which she sent in the post to me before I left me home in Ireland, are in me luggage. Which is lost. Can ye be a megastar and open the door? I'll give her a ring if she's got a landline once we get inside."

Eyes narrowing, Nancy looked Mary-Margaret up and down.

"Or shall I just lay meself down here and have a wee nap in the hall whilst I wait for her to get home?"

Ach, I shoulda brought me crutches. If I was teeterin' on them now, I'd already be inside havin' a peek.

"You look respectable enough," Nancy finally said with a nervous laugh. "Wait here and I'll be back with the key."

* * *

While she couldn't be one hundred percent sure, that haircut made Mary-Margaret believe that the man standing no more than a stone's throw away, fumbling with his keys, was the same man who had pushed past her just a few moments ago. Either that, or bowl cuts were making an unfortunate return to fashion.

"Excuse me," Mary-Margaret said, "but ye almost knocked me to me knees, did ye."

"Humph," he replied as he shoved the key into the lock, pushed the door open, and disappeared.

Drugs, she thought. Must have popped out to buy or sell drugs. I'll have to let me Michael know about this.

"Here. I think this is it," Nancy said, returning with a key on a yellow fob.

"Well, if not, I don't suppose rappin' on the lad next door's door would do us any good," Mary-Margaret replied with a grimace.

"On, you mean Mr. Fisher? No. I don't believe so. He's almost as new as me. Likely doesn't know Jane Ann, although we're a pretty tight-knit group here."

"And yet he wouldn't know his own neighbor? How's that, then?"

"Most of the tenants have been here a long time. Co-ops, the good ones, tend to be like that. People live here because they like each other, not just because it's affordable. And usually, you can't get in unless everyone agrees on you. But, from what I've been told, Mr. Fisher was a bit of an exception. It's kind of a sad story, really. He was dating—Oh," Nancy said, stopping herself, "I'm sorry. I don't think I should be disclosing personal information about the tenants."

"'Tis alright, luv. Not like I'm from around here," Mary-Margaret said. "So ye were sayin'?"

"His girlfriend used to live in a unit down the hall, and she, um, died."

"In his arms?"

"No. She was found in a ravine."

"How truly tragic," Mary-Margaret said. *Hanged herself if she was stuck with that one, no doubt.*

"Yes, well, a lot of people took pity on Mr. Fisher, and here he is."

"Moved into her place, did he?"

"No. We have a legacy policy here, and she had a sister who wanted the place. He'd just put his name on the list, and should have been at the bottom, but, when this place came up, they all felt sorry for him, so he was offered the unit. From what I've seen, let's just say Mr. Fisher doesn't fit the usual profile of our community."

"And how's that?"

"Between you and me, he kind of gives me the creeps."

"The lad almost mowed me down as I was comin' in. And then, not a few minutes later, didn't I see him just at his door, lookin' at me like he'd never seen me before."

"I'm not surprised. He's odd. He's always coming and going, so much so that it's hard not to notice. And he let you in, did he? That's against the co-op rules. Says so on the door. No one is allowed in unless you live here or are visiting someone."

"Which I am," Mary-Margaret quickly pointed out, not wanting to fall out of favor with someone so valuable.

"But they are the ones that have to buzz you in. I can't allow strangers to just barge in. Anyone else would have challenged you if they had seen you at the door. But not Mr. Fisher. I'll have to put up a bigger sign on the door."

"Well, there's always one, isn't there?" Mary-Margaret said with a feigned smile of understanding, her impatience growing.

After a moment of uncomfortable silence, Nancy said, "Now, let's get you inside, shall we?"

The younger of the two women knocked loudly on the door. They both waited quietly, and then Nancy knocked again.

"Luv, if me sister was inside, we wouldn't be standin' out here at this moment. I'm sure she would have heard ye and I talkin, recognized me voice and, knowin' that I was supposed to arrive yesterday, cursed herself for havin' forgot, and then opened the door to me."

"I know. It's just...you know."

Mary-Margaret looked at the closed door, and then, seeing that Nancy was not making any move to open the door, let out a loud sigh.

"Perhaps I'd be best to just set me weary bones down right here and now and wait for me sister. Or see if yer Mr. Fisher would be so kind as to let me lay me carcass on his couch until she returns."

The left corner of Nancy's mouth twitched, and then put her hand on the door handle. With more of a nervous shudder than an intentional twist of the knob, she opened the door. To both women's surprise, it was unlocked.

"Oh my." Nancy gasped, raising her hand to her mouth.

"You mean this isn't normal, luv?" Mary-Margaret asked, trying to sound calm while poking her head around Nancy to get a better look inside the ransacked apartment.

A quick scan showed one big room that was divided by an island with a small open kitchen on one side and a living room on the other. There were a couple of open doors along the wall to the right of the entrance that Mary-Margaret assumed led to a bedroom and a bathroom.

The cushions from the couch had been thrown to the floor and the lamps on both end-tables had been knocked off. One was shattered, the other salvageable. The curtain on the window over the kitchen sink had been torn down.

But no sign of Jane Ann.

"Not normal at all," Nancy said as she stepped into the apartment. "Neither was leaving the door unlocked like that. We are a co-op, but still...Jane Ann? Jane Ann?"

"I think ye had better stay out in the hall," Mary-Margaret said, pushing the superintendent back as she stepped past to get a better look inside. "Me son is a police detective, and he's always tellin' me about how so many crime scenes are—"

"Crime scenes?"

"Well, I'm just sayin'...the place bein' in shambles and all."

"You're right. We've got to call the police." Nancy agreed, steadying herself in the hallway. "I'm new here, and I don't want trouble." Nancy waited, cell phone at her ear, for the 9-1-1 operator to pick up.

"It might be more than a bit of trouble ye are reportin'," Mary-Margaret said as she stepped back into the living room. "No need for ye to have a look, luv, but I think somethin' terrible has happened."

Chapter Six

"Decided to join us, did you?" Father Miguel asked as he saw Mary-Margaret returning to the church. "Laura-Jean McQueen has just left. She got through all of the boxes you had laid out from yesterday as well as today's and most of tomorrow's. If only there were more parishioners like Laura-Jean."

"Can I have a moment, Father?" Mary-Margaret said, ignoring his praise of the daft woman.

He paused. "A moment?"

"Yes. I've got somethin' to tell ye."

He paused again. In the five long years since he had come to St. Francis's, Mary-Margaret had never had something to tell him that he wanted to hear. He doubted this would be any different.

"Certainly. My office?"

"Brill. Let me just put on a kettle, and I'll see you in the shake of a lamb's tail."

* * *

Father Miguel sat at his desk for what felt like the longest five minutes of his life. What on earth could Mary-Margaret O'Shea have to tell him? And why would he want to listen?

"Ach, Father, it's Jane Ann Hill." Mary-Margaret finally appeared, dropping herself into the chair across from his desk. "She's been murdered."

"Murdered?"

"Yes, Father. Murdered. I saw it with me own two eyes. Her bathroom...the bathtub looked like—ach, no need to go into it. Ye know what I'm sayin', I'm sure?"

She looked unflinchingly at the priest.

"No, I don't," he replied, narrowing his eyes. "Let's start from the beginning."

"I left Laura-Jean McQueen here to do the sortin' and went to Jane Ann's apartment. When I got there, she wasn't answerin' her door, so I got the super to let me in, and there I saw it—more blood and guts than I've ever seen in me life. I'm sure she's been murdered, Father. I know it." Mary-Margaret nodded with certainty, then took a big sip of her tea.

Now it was Father Miguel's turn to look unflinchingly at his problematic parishioner.

"Did ye hear me, Father?" Mary-Margaret raised her voice in case he hadn't.

"Yes, unfortunately," he replied, biting his lip.

"She's been murdered in her bathtub, Father."

"Let's," Father Miguel took a breath, "start again."

"With all due respect, Father, are ye dim? What part did ye miss?"

"The part where you went over to Jane Ann's apartment."

"It's a co-op, truth to be told. I know yer records have her livin' at that fancy condo downtown, but she doesn't. When she gets back, be sure to tell The New Girl to keep on top of the contact information. Clearly, it's important. Anyway, there I was, at this co-op—"

"And you saw her body in the bathtub?"

"No."

"Did you see *any* body in the bathtub?"

"No."

"But you did see a lot of...how did you put it...blood and guts."

"Father, with all due resp—"

"Have the police been called?"

"Of course, they have."

"And they have said—"

"Ach, I can't say," Mary-Margaret took another big gulp of tea."

"And why is that?"

"Because I don't actually know."

Father Miguel nodded slowly.

"Because I was high-tailin' it back here while they were goin' there, don'tcha know." she concluded with a nod.

"You didn't think they might have wanted to talk to you?" Father Miguel suggested slowly.

"Me Michael is a detective, if ye recall, Father. They know how to find me."

"Your Michael is one of many detectives, Mary-Margaret," he corrected. "And they might not know how to find you. Did you leave your name with anyone?"

"Well, Nancy knows me, of course."

"Who is Nancy?"

"The superintendent at the co-op, Father. Were ye not listenin' to me story at all, or is the logic behind it too complicated for yer mind to unravel in this moment?"

"Not that I'm doubting your abilities to relay information accurately, Mary-Margaret," Father Miguel said, ignoring the slight as he leaned back in his chair, "but did you give her your name and contact information?"

"Of course, I did...." She stopped short. "Not. She thinks I'm Jane Ann's sister."

"Pardon me?"

"Well, ye see, I needed to get—"

"Wanted to get," Father Miguel corrected.

"No need to cloud the issue with facts now, Father. As I was sayin', I needed to get into Jane Ann's apartment, but I thought it was locked, as anyone would, and I didn't have a key, so I told the super that I was her sister and—"

"She didn't notice that you have a strong foreign accent?"

"Irish. Not foreign," Mary-Margaret corrected. "And I told her that I had just arrived this minute from Ireland, lost me luggage that had the key that

29

Jane Ann had given me to her apartment, and—"

"Since retiring from the church, Mary-Margaret, you seem to have developed quite the knack for lying. Or," Father Miguel said with a smirk, "have you always had this gift?"

"Father, it's not at all like that. As ye well know, God forgives those that—"

"Lie? Steal? No, if I recall correctly, He isn't good with that sort of thing. Took up two of the ten command—"

"Father, if ye are goin' to be preachin' at me, rest assured that I'll be here on Sunday to hear the whole sermon. In the meantime, we have got to find Jane Ann's killer."

"We don't know that there is a killer to be found because we don't know that Jane Ann is dead. And, in the off chance that she is, we most certainly don't have to find her killer, if there even is one. She may have had some sort of medical emergency, and is now in the hospital. Have you considered that? Regardless, we don't have to do anything. You, on the other hand, have got to call the police and tell them everything you were going to tell me. Starting with your name."

"I was just goin' to do that, Father, after I finished me tea."

Taking a deep breath, she stood up.

"Oh, and by the way, how's that foot of yours?"

"A bit tender, now that ye mention it. Which reminds me, I've got to get out to me yoga. Very good for injury as well as maintainin' yer strength, so they say. Missed me usual class, but I'm sure they've got somethin' on this afternoon. Given the time, I'll likely be gone for the rest of the day."

"You can take the week if you wish. Laura-Jean has said she'll be back tomorrow and that she can handle the bazaar. Ashleigh will be back from her honeymoon after that. Can I see you to the door?"

"Thank ye, no, Father. I can see me own way out. And over me own dead body will Laura-Jean McQueen take over me bazaar, which ye called me back to run, lest ye forget."

"I have certainly not forgotten, Mary-Margaret," the priest said, biting his lip. "Have you heard from Jane Ann's daughter?"

"Chrystal? No, why?"

"Perhaps you could reach out to her?"

"And why would I do that?"

"Reachin' out to the congregation is yer bailiwick, Father. And I'm off to me yoga before me whole body seizes. Given how ye have taken to bitin' that lip, ye might want to consider comin' with me."

"Thank you, no," he said, inhaling deeply. "I suspect that whatever is ailing me will resolve itself in a very few days."

"Suit yerself, Father," Mary-Margaret said, and then thought: Yoga me foot. There's nothin' for it but to speak to me Michael now.

Chapter Seven

Mary-Margaret called Michael and insisted that he meet her for lunch at O'Leary's. Luckily, he was only required for a short time in court that day and was able to meet her before starting his evening shift. She was just about to open the door to the pub when she remembered that she had forgotten her crutches. She raced back around the corner to the church and then back to the pub, crutches in hand. She paused for a moment at the front door to put one under each arm and then made her way slowly into the half-empty room.

"Don't notice me out of breath," she told her son before she sat down at the tiny round table, laying down the crutches beside her. "I've been runnin' five beats to the four all mornin', what with the bazaar comin' on Saturday. Not at all easy with a broken foot, as ye can imagine. On top of that, can ye believe that Father Miguel actually thought that dope Laura-Jean McQueen could run the bazaar on her own? He has no idea how much work is involved."

"I'm sure he doesn't. So what was it you wanted to discuss?"

"Jane Ann Hill's murder. I've got information that ye will be wantin' in order to solve the case."

"Whoa. First off, who is Jane Ann Hill? And secondly, I don't solve murders."

"Didn't ye solve one just a few weeks ago, me son?"

"Yes, I did. But that wasn't my case. I was just assisting." He quickly glanced at the menu on the chalkboard by the bar as the server loomed over them. The pub filled up with the late-lunch crowd, and the server didn't look like she suffered fools lightly. "I'll have a pint of Guinness and your special. Mom?"

"Oh, just a crown float for me, luv. Half pint. And just a wee sandwich. I can see that yer new here. Tell them in the kitchen that it's for Mary-Margaret. They'll know what I want."

The server looked questioningly at Mary-Margaret for a moment before Michael gave her a slight nod, and she turned back towards the bar.

"You do know," he said, leaning across the table towards his mother, "that they can't make a half a pint of a crown float, don't you? I mean, they can, but they likely have to spoil the other half of the Strongbow."

"Since when were ye a bartender? Maybe there's someone else who'd like half a pint, and then we're grand, aren't we? And are we here to talk about how O'Leary's runs their business, or are we goin' to talk about a murder?"

"Go ahead, Mom." Michael cleared his throat and leaned back in his chair.

"As I was tryin' to say, Jane Ann Hill is a parishioner at St. Francis. She was missin' from me sortin' yesterday, which is not like her. So I said to Father Miguel—"

"Mom, I do have to get in to work this afternoon."

"No wonder ye are just a district detective. No patience, have ye? So, I dropped by Jane Ann's place today. Lovely little apartment in a co-op. Yer lads are probably there right now."

"Why?"

"Because I found the murder scene, and Nancy called it in."

"How is it you're able to get to all of these places with a broken ankle?"

"Foot."

"And who is Nancy?"

"Ye would be amazed to know what I can actually do, me son. And Nancy is the super at the co-op."

"And how do you know it's a murder scene? Did you see a body?"

"Ach, have ye been drinkin' from the same chalice as Father Miguel, me son? Trust me when I tell ye: there is no way anyone could make such a mess of the jacks as that and walk away."

"So where's the body?"

"Do I look like our Mandy, me lad?" Mary-Margaret said, throwing her

33

hands up in the air. "'Tis it not enough that I found the scene of the crime?"

"Thankfully, you are not at all like Detective Amanda Black. Regardless, I think you should be talking to Homicide about this."

"Well, I'm talkin' to ye right now. They can wait. Here's me tip for ye: Jane Ann Hill was murdered in the bathtub."

"Thanks for that, Mom."

"It may seem like nothin' now, but it will be somethin' later. Ta, luv," she said as the server placed their order on the table. She lifted her glass. "Sláinte!"

Michael raised his glass, then suddenly put his hand to his chest.

"Lad, ye aren't having the Big One, are ye? Shall I call the paramedics?"

"No, Mom. It's my cell phone vibrating. Probably Ron Roberts. I'll check for a message later."

"Our Ronnie? How is he? Is retirement suitin' him? Ach, I suppose not, what with Marie being so sick and all. She hasn't...." Mary-Margaret made a slashing motion across her neck.

"Not yet, but soon. Ron spends pretty much all of his time at the hospice with her now."

"Ach, such a shame. And he bein' such a good detective. Do ye think he'll come back after she..." Mary-Margaret made the slashing motion again.

"Dies? Unlikely. And it doesn't quite work that way anyway. Once you retire, you retire."

"Wouldn't be surprised if a lad like that goes into business for himself. Ron Roberts, Gentleman Detective. I can see it now."

Michael's cell phone vibrated again. This time, he pulled it from his jacket pocket and checked the message.

"I'm sorry, Mom, but I've got to go."

"I've not even begun to tell ye—"

"Mom," Michael began, shoveling forkfuls of meat pie into his mouth before washing every other bite down with a gulp of Guinness, "I'm hopeful that your Juliette—"

"Jane Ann," Mary-Margaret corrected.

"Jane Ann wasn't murdered, but if she was, I'm sure that whoever conducts the investigation will do a thorough job. Make sure you let the investigators know what you saw. Otherwise, stay out of it."

"So ye are not even goin' to look into it, then?"

"No."

"Not even pull the report once it's done?"

"No."

"Well, can ye at least print a copy out for me?"

"Absolutely not."

"Well, then...."

The words hung heavily between mother and son as Mary-Margaret gave Michael a long, unblinking look.

"I have to go, Mom," Michael said, washing down the last mouthful with his beer.

"I'm sure ye do. Enjoy yer police work, then. And don't worry about me. I'll just go off and catch this killer meself."

"Mom, let it go," Michael said, wiping his chin with his napkin. "You are not a homicide investigator, and you'll just get in the way."

"I see. Well, if that's what ye are thinkin'," she said, reaching down to pull her crutches up from beside her, "then I'll be on me way. Now, if ye will excuse me, I've got me book club tonight, so there'll be no dinner waitin' for ye when ye get home. Max is out for his supper at a lad from school's house but will likely be home by the time ye are in. If not, he'll be givin' ye a call to pick him up. But I suppose ye already knew all of that, bein' a Big City Detective and all. In any event, I don't want to be in the way, so I'm assumin' ye shall settle up with our server, or are ye too busy to take yer mam out for but a sip of beer and a dried sandwich?"

With a flourish, Mary-Margaret pushed her chair back from the table and, bashing her crutches on more chairs than necessary, maneuvered herself out of the pub.

Michael responded to the message on his phone, then dropped two twenties on the table to cover the thirty-dollar bill and left.

Chapter Eight

Mary-Margaret disliked being late, particularly when there was no reason for it. The outcome of her lunch with Michael had so annoyed her that she went for a very long walk without the crutches to clear her head. And now she was late for her book club and would have to stand—teetering on her crutches, no less—at the back of the room until she could make her way to her usual seat without looking like a complete fool.

"Tonight, as a special guest," Willow Anderson gushed, "we have the author of our book selection, *Woman at the Window*, joining us. As well as being an author, he's a retired detective inspector from the London Metropolitan Police. Please join me in welcoming Dexter Regan."

A wave of oooohs and ahhhhhs mixed with the applause as the fifteen members of the St. Francis of Assisi Book Club welcomed the man standing before them. Mary-Margaret took advantage of this distraction to make her way from the back of the room to her customary spot in the front row.

"Thank you. As you can imagine, I'm as thrilled to be here as you appear to be at having me," the trim gentleman said before sitting on the chair provided. "I'd like to thank my daughter, Abby, for recommending *Woman at the Window* to you and for making arrangements for me to be here to talk about it during our family visit."

Everyone clapped politely as Abby Regan smiled and gave a little wave to her father.

"We've not got much time, so let's dive in, shall we?" Regan said, holding up a copy of his book while taking a sip of water from the glass on the table beside him. "I write police procedurals because I know police procedures. Some things may be a bit different here, I suppose, but policing is fundamentally the same in every Western country. I'm assuming you've read the book, and Abby tells me you've got some questions prepared, so let's just dive in. Yes, you."

"When you wrote the book, was it based on anything you've ever done, or is it all just fiction?" a newcomer to the club asked.

"Good question. Everything I write is based on my own understanding and interpretation of what I've done, which is to say, it's fiction. Anyone else?" he said, scanning the small group before settling on Mary-Margaret. "Yes?"

"Yer main character lives with his mother. How realistic is that?" she asked.

"Well, cost of living is quite high in London, and our man doesn't make that much money—"

"Seems he spends more of it than he earns, is what you mean," Alice Kerr, a founding member of the club, called out.

A nervous chuckle made its way through the small gathering.

"Either way," the author said with a sniff, "he can't afford to live on his own in London on just a policeman's salary."

"Do ye think his mother helps him solve the crimes?" Mary-Margaret asked.

"No. Not at all."

"That doesn't ring true, does it?" she said, looking behind her for support. "I mean, she's there listenin' to what he has to say throughout the book. Wouldn't it make sense that she might have some insight into the crime?"

Regan cleared his throat.

"Unless, of course, she's just ornamental. Eye-candy, like?" Mary-Margaret added.

A few of the younger women laughed.

"This is where the fact part of fiction comes in, Mrs...?"

"O'Shea. Mary-Margaret O'Shea." She stood up.

"Yes. Well, you see, Mrs. O'Shea, solving crime in real life is quite challenging. Not at all like it is on TV, and it takes years of training and experience to reach the point where—"

"So ye are sayin' that a lay person couldn't truly understand the complexities of a real criminal investigation?"

"Exactly."

"That the logic behind it would be too complicated for the average person's mind to unravel."

"Correct."

"But a trained policeman could?"

"Yes. That's what I'm saying."

"Have ye met me son? Michael. He's a detective as well."

The retired detective inspector just smiled politely.

"Mary-Margaret, perhaps we could let someone else...?" Willow Anderson said, letting her words hang.

"Of course," Mary-Margaret said, sitting down.

* * *

"Thank ye for coming to pick me up, Arthur," Mary-Margaret said. "I really appreciate it. If it wasn't for ye, there'd be no way I could get out and about to me book club and the like. Although," she added, looking at the condition of the car as she opened the passenger door, "are ye sure this thing is roadworthy?"

"Not completely, but it'll get us to your place. Here, give me your crutches. I'll put them in the back seat."

"Don't forget I'm still at me Michael's."

"Right. Okay. Well, in that case, we might be in for a bit of a ride."

"Perhaps I should just take the bus..." She looked out the window, hoping to see one coming.

Arthur Lukowitz was the cleaner the agency had sent over a few years back when Mary-Margaret had gallstones, and Michael thought she might need some help around the house. The gallstones passed, and Arthur stayed, not so much because she needed any help—because if she did, Arthur was certainly not the one to offer it—but because she had taken a shine to him.

Likely a gangly boy, Arthur had somehow morphed into a paunchy thirty-six-year-old man who rented a room in a tiny apartment from some woman he had met online. Aside from his lack of cleaning ability, he had poor time-management and interpersonal skills. His hygiene, depending on a number of variables, could also be questionable at times. But he had a good heart and Mary-Margaret quite liked him. Not at this moment, however.

"Arthur! Stay in yer lane, luv!" she screamed, her hands on the dashboard, bracing for impact.

"Sorry, MM, I was a bit distracted," Arthur said, giving the steering wheel a sharp pull to miss the oncoming car before braking abruptly to avoid rear-ending the bus Mary-Margaret was beginning to wish she was on. "My mind was on this conference that I've been trying to organize all week. It's making me crazy. Most people don't even call me back."

"I hear ye, luv," she said, releasing her grip and giving her neck a rub. "Everyone loves a conference, but nobody loves to help."

To look at Arthur, Mary-Margaret figured, one might assume many things about him, including homelessness, friendlessness, and perhaps more than one mental health issue. Any one of the aforementioned possibilities would make him seem like a terrible candidate for a cleaner for an older woman living alone. While some of these assumptions might be true—although which were true could vary at any given time—the two had become great friends.

"And the people who do call me back are useless."

"In yer lane, Arthur. Mind the road ahead," she warned, noticing the car begin to swing into oncoming traffic again. "And if ye don't mind me askin', do ye possess a driver's license by any chance?"

"Almost."

"Which means…?"

"I passed the written test, but I never got around to doing the road test."

"I see."

"Does it show?"

"Oh, just barely, I'm sure. Listen, luv. Once we get to Michael's, ye may want to consider just parkin' the car and takin' the bus home. Yer friend can come 'round and pick it up later, perhaps."

"Let's just see how it goes."

Suddenly, she reached over and grabbed the steering wheel. She pushed it up sharply, then pulled it down again to avoid hitting the cyclist in front of them.

"This isn't going very well, is it, MM?"

"No, luv. I definitely think ye should take the bus home."

They drove the rest of the way in silence: one ostensibly concentrating on the road, the other praying that her life would not end in a fiery crash.

"Would ye like to come in for a cuppa before ye head out, then, lad?" she asked after he abruptly stopped the car in the middle of the road by Michael's house.

"I'd love to, MM, but I've got—"

"No need to explain anythin' to me, luv. I'm assumin' ye'll actually park the car before ye go, though."

"Oh. Right."

Chapter Nine

"Detective O'Shea. How may I help you?"

"Michael, 'tis yer mother."

"Is everything okay?"

"Grand, luv. I was at me book club, and then Arthur came by to pick me up, on account of me broken foot and all, and then he dropped me home, and we had a —"

"You do know I'm at work, right, Mom?"

"Of course I do, Michael. I called ye, remember? Honestly, luv, I don't think ye should be back at work so soon. Clearly, ye are not right in the head yet."

"Is there anything I can help you with?"

"Ach, yes. Can ye call the morgue and see if they have any Jane Does there?"

"No."

"Michael, this is police business."

"Exactly, so let's leave it to the police."

"So what I am hearin' with me own ears is that ye would rather sit on yer duff than make a single phone call for yer mother that would identify a murder victim."

"No. What I am saying is—"

"Never mind. Arthur and I will sort it ourselves."

"You haven't dragged him into this, have you, Mom?"

"He offered."

"What's that barking in the background?"

"Wee Phil. He has to go out to the jacks. I'll get Max to take him for a walk 'round."

"And that's another thing. Why is Sally's dog at our house?"

"I've told ye before, but clearly the logic behind it is too complicated for yer mind to unravel in this moment."

"Clearly. Okay, here's the deal. Let me pull up the report on Jane Ann Hill. If there are no updates, then—"

"Well, of course, there'll be no updates because no one has bothered to identify her cold body at the morgue. Now, if ye were to make that call, ye could be the one to give this investigation a good kick."

"I've got enough on my plate already, Mom. I don't need to make work."

"I see. Well then, if investigatin' a murder is too much for ye, I'll ring off now and take wee Phil for a piddle."

"Get Max to do it. You've got to watch your foot."

"Me foot is fine!"

"I thought it was broken."

"'Tis."

"So get Max to take the dog out. Meanwhile, keep your nose out of the Jane Ann Hill investigation."

"Michael, where did that come from?"

"I'm going to make this as clear as I can: I'll find the name of the lead investigator for the missing persons case for you. Tomorrow morning after you get home from church, I want you to call that investigator and tell him—"

"Or her—"

"Or her how you came to be in Jane Ann Hill's apartment. Tell them the whole story, Mom, as crazy as it sounds. And then hang up the phone, have a cup of tea, and do whatever it is that you do on Sunday afternoons."

"As if makin' a whole spread for ye lot isn't enough to do on a Sunday afternoon."

"That's not what I meant, Mom. What I do mean is: do not go back to her apartment—"

"Co-op."

"Co-op. Do not call her daughter."

"About her daughter. Seemed very vague about her mother's habits."

"Not everyone's mother lives with them, Mom."

"Ye are lucky to have me."

"And do not call Frank at the morgue—"

"I would never do such a thing."

"Yes, you would. Don't. I'm going to hang up the phone now, Mom. I'll leave the name and number of that investigator for you on the kitchen table when I get home. It's busy here, and with Ron gone, I'm on my own until Carla Hagenauer gets transferred in."

"Carla? Well now, that will be new for ye, son. Ye have not had a girl partner since ye were in the squad all those years ago."

"Speaking of which, Julia Vendramini has just come in for her shift. She's waving to you."

"Hello, Julia," Mary-Margaret hollered into the receiver. "How is yer Keith? Still have the dogs, luv?"

"She can't hear you, Mom. You're on the phone with me."

"Right."

"I'm going to hang up now, Mom."

"Good night, Michael. And be safe. I'm saying a wee prayer for ye, as I do every night. And Julia."

Chapter Ten

"I'm surprised to see you here," Laura-Jean McQueen said as Mary-Margaret waltzed into what she still considered her office.

"And I could say the same of ye. Mind?" Mary-Margaret pushed past the marginally younger woman, switching on the kettle on her way to hanging her coat up on the coat tree in the back corner of the room. "And can ye get out of me chair?"

"Father Miguel thought that coming back was too much for you," Laura-Jean replied, not moving.

"Well, it's not. Excuse me." Mary-Margaret stepped towards what was still, for the time being, her desk, pushing past Laura-Jean again to put her purse in the bottom drawer.

Laura-Jean remained seated, staring at her nemesis, who maneuvered around her.

"Out!" Mary-Margaret roared, barely giving Laura-Jean a moment to move before plopping herself down in the chair.

"Where are your crutches?" Laura-Jean asked, leaning against the doorframe, more for balance than effect.

"What crutches?"

"The ones you've been carrying around since you got here."

"Oh, Jesus, Mary, and Joseph. I've left them in the back of Arthur's car." Mary-Margaret looked around her, as if the crutches might just happen to be next to her coat or, somewhat less likely, under the desk.

"So your foot isn't broken," Laura-Jean said, straightening up.

"'Tis," Mary-Margaret said, content that her crutches were, in fact, in the back of the car Arthur had picked her up in last night, "but I'm healin'. Quickly."

Laura-Jean pursed her lips.

"Sortin' this morning, are we? Brill. Best be on yer way, then."

"You don't work here anymore, you know," Laura-Jean said without taking her eyes off the older woman.

"Well, that's up for debate, isn't it?"

"Ashleigh will be back on Monday and—"

"Until then, I'm steerin' this ship. Now if ye'll be on yer way…"

Laura-Jean twitched and was about to say something when a young woman tapped on the open door.

"Have you come to sort?" Laura-Jean asked with a crocodile smile.

"Ach, no, Laura-Jean. This is the daughter of our lapsed parishioner. And a clear example of why ye should not be runnin' anythin'." Mary-Margaret turned to Chrystal. "Any word, luv?"

Chrystal's eyes welled up with tears, and she began to sob.

"Oh, me lamb. What is it?" Mary-Margaret said, taking the distraught woman into her arms.

"The police called. Said they want me to meet them at the morgue as soon as I can get there. They think—"

Michael did heed me advice, then. Smart lad, is me son.

"I know it's a lot to ask, but there's no one else," Chrystal added between sobs, her runny nose and tears soaking the shoulder of Mary-Margaret's blouse. "Can you come with me?"

Mary-Margaret looked past Chrystal towards Laura-Jean.

"Of course, I will, me lamb. This is exactly what a church secretary does, past or present."

"Thank you so much," Chrystal said, wiping her nose as she pulled away from Mary-Margaret. "I'm just parked out front."

"I'll grab me purse."

"Won't you need your crutches?" Laura-Jean asked with a smirk.

"I told ye. I'm a fast healer," Mary-Margaret said as she followed Chrystal out of the office.

"Your foot isn't broken. That's why you don't need those crutches."

"Laura-Jean McQueen!" Mary-Margaret stopped dead in her tracks, turning back to address her directly. "This is neither the time nor the place to be havin' such a conversation. And to think Father Miguel thought ye could take over from me. Ach. Chrystal, I'm right behind ye, luv."

* * *

The glass front doors of the morgue opened, and the two women walked over to the security desk just inside. A slight unpleasant odor of something she didn't recognize aggravated Mary-Margaret's nose. It was not exactly as Frank had described it to her, although she was willing to accept that the part of the morgue that he saw was not like the area that was open to the public.

"Chrystal Hill, I presume?" a man wearing a dark suit that hung loosely off his thin frame asked. Without waiting for a response, he continued. "I'm Detective Billy Gill. Thank you for coming in." He turned to Mary-Margaret. "And you are…?"

"Mary-Margaret O'Shea. Michael's mother," she said, taking in a deep breath as she drew herself up to her full height of five foot two.

"Michael…?"

"O'Shea. Detective Michael O'Shea. I'm sure ye know him."

"I'm sure. So, Chrystal, you know why you're here, no doubt. I'm assuming you've brought your friend along for support. Do you want her to come in for the identification?"

"Of course she does, lad. Why else would she be bringin' me along? For a wee bit of craic? Hardly. Ye are certainly no Mandy, are ye?"

"Excuse me, Miss…? Mrs…?"

"O'Shea. Mrs. O'Shea. Mary-Margaret—"

"Yes. Well, what we are investigating now may be a homicide."

Chrystal slumped into Mary-Margaret.

"Not much of a bedside, have ye?"

"Perhaps not. Regardless, do you want Mrs. O'Shea to come with you to identify the body, Ms. Hill?"

Chrystal nodded.

"Come with me, then. Both of you."

I'll have to have a word with me Michael about this one. Horrible man. Shouldn't be allowed to speak to the public at all.

Chrystal and Mary-Margaret followed the investigator down the hall into a room that looked very much like a living room, complete with a flat-screen TV on the wall. Detective Gill motioned to the two women to sit on the couch facing the screen as he picked up a remote control from the end table. Before they could get settled, the screen was already flashing on.

A woman's face appeared, a white blanket covering her neck. Her eyes were closed and she looked very calm, as if she was asleep. For a moment, Mary-Margaret could almost forget that they were looking at the face of a dead woman. And then she heard Chrystal begin to weep. The weeping quickly became soul-wrenching sobs. And still, the image of the dead woman remained on the screen.

"Recognize her?" Detective Gill asked.

"Clearly, she does," Mary-Margaret stated.

"Recognize her?" he repeated.

"Yes. Sh-she's my mother."

And with that, the floodgates opened, and Chrystal began to wail in earnest.

"For the record, can you state your mother's full name, please?" the detective said over her cries.

"J-j-jane Ann H-i-i-i-ill-l-l-l-l."

"Thank you," he said, pressing a button on the remote, causing the screen to go blank. He straightened his tie before reaching for the door handle. "Take as long as you need. There is Kleenex on the end table there."

"No bedside at all," Mary-Margaret muttered as she consoled the murdered woman's daughter.

* * *

"'Tis a terrible thing," Mary-Margaret began, holding the weeping woman.

"I'm an orphan now," she cried.

"Oh, luv," Mary-Margaret said, shaking her head. "So ye've no da either?"

"No. He passed away two years ago."

"Ach, that's not long at all, is it now?"

"No," she sobbed.

"And yer parents were separated, weren't they?"

"Divorced."

"Really? And ye lived with yer mam, then?"

"No. She was a bit of a …wild card."

"A wild card? Our Jane Ann? She was a devout—"

"She wasn't always," Chrystal said. "I mean, there were a few years when I didn't see her at all."

"So ye haven't known yer mother all along?" Wait until I tell me Michael this. A mother knows.

"No. We had a sort of an…estrangement…for a long time. We just began to get to know each other again over the past couple of years, around the time when Dad got sick. Just before he died."

Chrystal burst into tears.

"Ach, me lamb," Mary-Margaret said, cradling the younger woman against her body, rubbing her back. "'Tis the way more often than not. Just when we start to find our feet again, the rug takes on a mind of its own."

"Oh, Mom. Why do you always make things so complicated?" Chrystal finally said, wiping her nose with her shirt sleeve. "I'm sorry. I really didn't mean to say that."

Mary-Margaret sat quietly.

"When I was little, my parents fought a lot, but I always felt that they both loved me."

"So it wasn't like fightin'. It was banterin'. Me and my Jimmy, God rest his soul, used to have some real—"

"My dad worked really hard. I mean *really* hard to make Mom's life good."

"And was it?"

"Was it what—good? I don't know. I thought so, but I guess I was wrong."

"Why is that, luv?"

"One day, my mom was gone. There was an envelope on the table addressed to my dad, and a note beside a snack for me on the counter telling me that she would always love me and that I would be fine."

"I see."

"It was not a good time in our lives."

"I can't imagine it would be."

"Dad took it really hard. I don't know what was in the envelope or what she said or if they spoke again, but I guess they must have because she came back."

"Came back as in—"

"Into our lives. Just like she'd never left. Even though she had been gone for what seemed like forever but was probably maybe a year or so. But there she was, on the front porch one afternoon, having a smoke—"

"Jane Ann smoked?"

"Like a chimney back then. And there she was," Chrystal continued, "pretending like no time had passed and that she'd just stepped outside for a few minutes. Except that she had to wait for someone to let her in because my dad had changed the locks."

"And did he let her back in?"

"No, he didn't. I did. I came home from school, and there she was. I let her in, and I think he just kind of went with it."

"That must have been quite a shock for ye."

"Sure was. But not as much of a shock as it was for my dad."

"I can imagine. So he took her back, then?"

"Surprisingly, yes. But she was gone for good six months later."

"I'm sorry, luv."

"Me, too."

"So it was just ye and yer da, then?"

"Yep. He raised me."

"Never remarried?"

"Nope. Said he was too busy looking after me to go out and find someone."

"And was he?"

"I don't think so. I think she broke his heart."

"So he carried a bit of a torch for yer mam?"

"I don't know. I used to think so. I wanted to believe so. You know—that romantic knight in shining armor thing where the guy pines forever."

"It does happen, ye know."

"Maybe."

"Did ye grow up near here?"

"Oh yes, just a few blocks from here, in the house we all lived together, before...."

Her voice trailed off.

"Funny, yer mam never spoke of him."

"I'm not surprised. In fact, I'm sure there's a lot you don't know about my mother."

"Well, like I said, we've all got a mystery or two in our pantries."

"Some more so than others," Chrystal said. "In the end, I think she gave up a lot."

"How so?"

"Well, me, for one. And a man who would do anything for her for a series of loser boyfriends. A good house in a good neighborhood to end up here."

"Well, we don't know the ins and outs of it all. Ye did say yer parents argued a lot. Maybe it wasn't such a happy home after all."

"Or maybe she just wasn't such a happy person after all."

"I suppose we'll never know. If she wasn't happy, I just hope she is now resting in God's company."

"Fat lot of good that'll do her, won't it?"

Mary-Margaret looked as if she'd just been slapped.

"I'm sorry. I just feel—I don't know what I feel. It's all just too much for me right now. I think I should go home."

"Then that's just what we'll do, luv."

* * *

Mary-Margaret flung her purse onto her former desk and flicked on the kettle. She reached for her mug, but it was gone. Glancing quickly around the office, a horrible thought crossed her mind.

If that Laura-Jean McQueen has taken me mug for her cuppa to do her sortin', I shall put a pox upon her, the results of which not even Father Brian himself could undo.

She felt her blood pressure rising. Between this and the trip to the morgue, there was nothing to do but to call Michael.

"Detective O'Shea. How may I help you?"

"Michael, it's yer mother."

"I'm not even going to ask."

"Well, ye needn't because I'm goin' to tell ye. I was just at the morgue—"

"I thought I—"

"With Chrystal Hill. Held her as she wailed at the sight of her dead mother. Do ye know Detective Billy Gilly?"

"Billy Gill. Yes. Why?"

"He is a horrible man and ought not to be allowed out in public. A disgrace, he is. I wish our Mandy was on the case."

"She can't be the officer in charge of every homicide, you know. And that reminds me: I have to get a statement done for her today for the Johnstone matter."

"Is that the name of the wastrel that tried to murder ye? There's nothin' for it, lad. Just show the judge the pictures of yer noggin that they took at the hospital, and they'll be throwin' that bucket of evil away forever. But while I've got ye on the line, son, did ye happen to notice a car parked out front of the house last night?"

"Yeah. It was leaking gas and oil and all sorts of crap onto the road. Had it towed. Truck driver said if anyone had walked by with a cigarette, we'd all have blown up."

"I see."

"Why do you ask?"

"No reason. Did ye happen to see anythin' inside the car?"

"I didn't look. Why?"

"No reason."

"I highly doubt that, but I really have to get back to work now unless there's anything else?"

"No, luv. Just called for a wee chat while I'm waitin' on me tea. I'll be ringin' off now. Bye-bye bye bye-bye-bye ."

And I'd be having that tea now if that Laura-Jean McQueen hadn't taken me mug. Oh, she will not hear the end of this! Steady, Mary-Margaret. Don't be gettin' yer knickers tied. Last thing ye need is to have Father Miguel find ye here, sprawled on the floor. Me body wouldn't even be cold before that daft Laura-Jean would be chuckin' me kettle and bringin' out the Keurig.

Mary-Margaret picked up the receiver of the church phone and poked a series of numbers, trying to take a couple of calm breaths while the phone rang at the other end.

"Detective Amanda Black. Homicide."

"Mandy, luv, it's Mary-Margaret O'Shea. Would ye be interested in goin' out for a bit of lunch today?"

"You know, besides my sister, you're the only person who calls me Mandy. And as a matter of fact, I could use something to eat," Amanda replied. "Let me just finish watching this security video, and I'll meet you at…O'Leary's, is it?"

"A girl after me own heart, are ye, Mandy. See ye within the hour?"

"My treat."

"Ach, how can it get any better than that?"

Mary-Margaret hung up the phone, and even though her purse was sitting on the desk right in front of her, opened the bottom right-hand drawer of her former desk out of habit. There, sitting where her purse would have been, was her mug.

Thanks be to the Good Lord and all that occupies the heavens above. I shall save me pox-to-end-all-poxes for another day.

Chapter Eleven

"I'll have a glass of your house white and the Caesar. And you?"

"Half crown float," Mary-Margaret said. "And a wee sandwich. Just tell the kitchen it's for Mary-Margaret. They'll know what to do."

The women passed their menus to the server who nodded at Amanda and smiled slightly at Mary-Margaret.

"New girl. Thinks I'm daft, does she." Mary-Margaret leaned in towards Amanda. "They'll set her straight at the bar. They always do."

"Thanks again for all of your help on the Sibby Mac case," Amanda said, looking over her shoulder at the server motioning to their table and the bartender nodding with a smile. "How's Mike's head after that last dust-up?"

"Ach, he's likely feeling a lot less than what he's lettin' on. Meanwhile, I'm pullin' straws to find ways to keep meself there to take care of him."

"Well, you can always come to my house."

"Ye are a luv, Mandy. But the reason I invited ye out wasn't to get a stopover at yer place. I need yer help."

"If it's anything to do with Mike, I can put in a call…"

The server set down a glass of white wine and a half-pint mug of crown float before making her way to another table.

"Sláinte. And no, nothin' like that. It's about a murder."

"Cheers. Murder's my game. Go."

"Me friend, Jane Ann Hill, was murdered."

"Yes. Billy Gill is the investigator assigned to the case."

"Oh, so ye know all about it, then?"

"Only that Billy Gill is in charge, that they haven't released the cause of death, and that he's content to treat this as a homicide investigation."

"Well, that's good news."

"What part?"

"That they're finally seein' this for what it is. Good."

"Billy's got a pretty good sixth sense on this sort of thing. Started as a missing persons investigation, but he took one look at the scene and decided that—"

"And that's exactly what I told me Michael," Mary-Margaret said, a huge smile on her face that quickly turned into a frown as she lowered her voice and leaned towards Amanda. "I have some information—"

"I'll give Billy a call and see when he's available to talk to you." Amanda reached down to pull her cell phone from her purse on the floor next to her chair.

"No, wait," the older woman said, sitting back in her chair. "I'd rather talk to ye."

"Thanks, Mary-Margaret, but it doesn't quite work that way. This is Billy's case and—"

"Off the record."

"Oh. Okay." Amanda slowly slid her phone back into her purse.

"It's like this: I was the one who got the superintendent at the co-op to open the door."

"Okay."

"And I was the one who saw the bathroom."

"I know nothing about the case, so this means nothing to me."

"Ach, Father Miguel was right. But don't ever tell him that. It's all the lies..." She looked down at the table as shamefaced as her nature permitted.

"Did you kill Jane Ann Hill?" Amanda asked, suppressing a smile.

"No!"

The server arrived with their food but stepped back, startled by the vehemence in Mary-Margaret's voice.

"Do you know who killed Jane Ann Hill?" Amanda continued, her expression a bit sterner.

"No."

"Did you tamper with any evidence?" Amanda's tone was serious now.

"Not that I know of."

"Then I don't care what you said to whom."

"Ach, that's such a weight off me heart."

The server set the plates down in front of the two women, gave a quick smile, and then retreated to the bar.

"So you entered the crime scene, which means your prints are everywhere. Might want to let Billy know so that Forensics can cross-reference you and rule you out as a suspect."

"Suspect to murder? Me Michael would chuck me out on me ear for sure if that were the case."

"And you saw the crime scene. This salad is amazing. Why haven't we been coming here every week?"

"I've no objection to it," Mary-Margaret said, picking up her sandwich, "although me figure might suffer."

"At your age—"

"And what age would that be? If 'twas said by anyone but ye, Mandy, I'd have up and walked out."

"And if it was anyone but you calling me Mandy, I'd have beat you to the door. After we finish lunch, why don't you let me run you over to HQ, and you can give a statement, and then if he needs anything else, Billy will call you."

"Me Michael also said I should give a statement. As long as it's not to that Billy Gilly—"

"Billy Gill."

"Horrible man. Ye should have seen the way he treated Jane Ann's poor orphaned daughter."

"Yes, he's not the warmest guy on the planet, but he's a helluva good investigator."

"At least he's got somethin' goin' for him, then."

The two women sat in silence for a few minutes, enjoying their meals.

"I'm wonderin', luv: What happens when a murder doesn't get solved?"

"I wouldn't know. That's never happened to me." Amanda laughed and took an almost lady-like sip of her wine. "If your sandwich was anything like my salad, the food here is quite good. If we had more time, and I wouldn't have to run an extra five K to make up for it tomorrow, I'd order a dessert. But what were you asking? Oh, right: the case stays with that investigator until it gets solved."

"What happens if he retires? Does it just get put on the shelf?"

"Depends. If it's a case where tips are still coming in, it remains active. Otherwise, it goes to Cold Cases."

"How many unsolved murders do ye have on yer plate at the moment?"

"None, remember? I solve all of mine."

Seeing their glasses almost empty, the server came by.

"Another round, ladies?"

"Not for me," Amanda said. "I'm on the clock, but don't let me hold you back, Mary-Margaret."

"No, luv, there's a reason why I only have half a pint. One day, I may even tell ye...when yer not on duty."

"Just the bill, then," Amanda said. "One bill. No rush."

The server nodded and walked away.

"Ach, I'm sorry, luv. Here's me calling ye out for lunch, and all we're doing is talkin' shop. How are yer girls?"

"One is pregnant, the other is not."

"Oh. A bit of a surprise, was it?"

"You could say that."

"And?"

"And what?"

"Sorry. Not me place to ask."

"She hasn't decided yet."

"And the da?"

"No idea."

Mary-Margaret tried not to give a disapproving look.

"She's not saying," Amanda said.

"Me manners. Not me business. Enjoyed yer salad, then, did ye? I've never been a salad eater. Not in me genes, I suppose."

The two spent the next five minutes chatting about less contentious matters and would have continued on had Amanda's cell phone not begun to ring non-stop.

"No rest for the wicked," Amanda said, catching the eye of the server, who seemed to have forgotten about them, and paying the bill. "I'll drive you to HQ."

"That would be lovely, Mandy. And if ye happen to run into him in yer travels, tell me Michael that I was on me crutches."

"I'm not even going to ask."

Chapter Twelve

By the time she left police headquarters, it was far too late to go back to the church, but Mary-Margaret didn't particularly want to rush home. She had forgotten the start and end times of Michael's various shifts and didn't want to run the risk of him seeing her without the only thing that was keeping her broken foot facade going—the crutches. Perhaps she would give Arthur a call this evening to see if the owner of the car had picked it up from whatever pound it had been towed to. Of course, it would have been easier to call Michael and have him follow up for her, but that would raise too much suspicion. Calling Mandy for such a trivial matter was out of the question. If only Ron Roberts was still around.

With nothing else to do, she hopped on the bus and went for a ride. It took her past the church, past the rundown inner-city neighborhoods, past the posh little bubble where Michael lived that was quickly becoming her new neighborhood, and finally into an up-and-coming neighborhood before looping back around.

Doing the same trip in reverse, she found herself smack dab in front of Jane Ann Hill's co-op. Remembering what Louise, her massage therapist, always said about there being no coincidences, Mary-Margaret got off the bus and approached a couple of officers who were standing together a few paces away from the front door of the building.

"Excuse me, Officers?"

"Yes?" the taller of the two replied.

"Yes. Well, I was wonderin—"

"Do you live here, ma'am?" the shorter one asked.

"No. Not exactly."

"Uh-huh. Well, unless you live here—"

"But me sister does. Did. Jane Ann Hill?"

The two officers looked at each other.

"I understand she's been murdered," Mary-Margaret continued with a slight sniffle. *Not gettin' involved. Just makin' sure things are bein' done properly.*

"Hang on a sec," the shorter one said, reaching for the mic clipped on his epaulet. "Tango-four-two-foxtrot to anyone on scene?"

"I've already been in her apartment. I'm the one who—"

"Go ahead, Tango-four-two-foxtrot."

"We've got the sister of your victim here. Do you want to talk to her?"

"Sister? That wouldn't happen to be Mary-Margaret O'Shea, would it?"

"I dunno. I'll check," the officer said, giving Mary-Margaret a questioning look.

"Yes, that would be me," she said, frowning. Clearly, the young detective from Homicide that Mary-Margaret had spoken to had wasted no time in relaying her information to his boss, Detective Gill.

"No. I'll come to you. Keep her there."

"10-4." The officer turned to Mary-Margaret. "The boss said—"

"I know, luv." She was now regretting that she had gotten off the bus. "I heard."

"Mrs. O'Shea," Detective Gill said as he approached her, "thank you for coming by so quickly."

Mary-Margaret nodded.

"Medeiros got in touch with you, did he? I'd asked him to give you a call and have you meet me here when he gave me the annotated version of the statement you gave him."

"He did not get in touch with me, nor did I make a statement," Mary-Margaret corrected.

"Well, you're here, which is the main thing, and what did you think that interview was all about?"

"Do ye mean that could be entered into a court of law?"

"It could be, yes."

"All of it?"

"Whatever is deemed relevant."

"Jesus, Mary, and Joseph," Mary-Margaret whispered, crossing herself. "The whole world will see what a liar I am. Father Miguel was right. No good can come of this."

"I doubt that your story about being her sister will be relevant by the time we come to trial," Detective Gill said, smiling over at the two uniformed officers. "And thank you for all of your suspect tips."

"Me pleasure."

"Between you and me, Mrs. O'Shea, I sincerely doubt, however, that the little neighbor would have the strength to kill anyone." He took a deep breath and then continued. "How well do you know Chrystal Hill?"

"The daughter? Are ye sayin' she did it?"

"I'm not saying anything. It just seems to me that, in the absence of anyone else—"

"So ye know her da is dead, then, do ye?"

"I did pick up a thing or two at detective school, Mrs. O'Shea," he said with a slight smile. "But about the daughter. As I see it, she's the one who will reap any financial gain from this."

"And just how much financial gain do ye think there will be comin' from this one?" Mary-Margaret said, motioning to the co-op. "I don't suppose they taught common sense at that detective school of yers?"

Detective Gill looked grandly at the co-op behind them.

"As I said, I appreciate your help. We've got it from here, thanks."

"Yer welcome," Mary-Margaret replied, not sure whether he was trying to take the mickey out of her or not. "But tell me, Billy Gilly—"

The two officers began to giggle. Detective Gill sighed.

"Detective, I meant."

"Not the first time I've heard that."

"Still…" *Ach, manners, luv!*

"I was named after my mother's brother," he explained. "I have a brother and a sister, you know."

"Do ye, now?"

"Named after my maternal grandparents. Philip and Mildred," he continued, cracking a slight smile.

Mary-Margaret thought about that for a moment, then, sensing he was taking the mickey out of her this time, said, "Go on out of that, then!"

"I do have a brother and a sister," he said, "but not named Philly and Milly. And everyone called me William until I went through basic training. Now, about your friend, Jane Ann Hi—"

"She's not me friend. She is...was...a member of our parish, but I've not seen her for a few years."

"Your commitment to assist in solving the murder of a relative stranger is noteworthy, Mrs. O'Shea. Walk with me. I have a few questions to ask about the scene."

He turned and strode back towards the co-op entrance, pausing to make sure that Mary-Margaret was following him.

"If I'm walking too quickly, let me know. I understand you have or have had a broken ankle?" He gave a conspiratorial wink.

Oh, me stars. This man knows everythin'. What if me Michael finds out from his police pals?

"Had an issue with me foot, as I told yer lad, yes, but I think I can keep up to ye."

"As you are well-aware," he said, stopping abruptly and turning towards her, "this is a homicide investigation, and, while you aren't currently under oath, I'm expecting you to be truthful. Deal?"

"Oh, absolutely."

"Excellent. Now, I will need you to point out any things in the apartment that you may have touched."

Mary-Margaret's step slowed as she took a deep breath.

"Don't worry. We aren't going to be looking in the bathroom. I'm assuming you didn't actually go in there?"

"No, I did not. I could see right enough what had happened from the doorway."

"Excellent."

Detective Gill waved off the officer standing at the entrance to the low-rise and then the officer standing in the hallway beside the door to Jane Ann Hill's apartment.

Mary-Margaret paused at the doorway long enough for Detective Gill to reconsider. "On second thought, we don't actually have to go in. It's a small place. I'm sure you can point out where you were from here."

He turned the doorknob and carefully pushed open the door.

"Hey!" a man in a white paper coverall with white booties over his shoes called out. "Oh, sorry, Billy. I didn't realize you'd be coming back in."

"Don't worry. I won't be. I just want the other woman who came into the apartment earlier to point out where she had been."

"Great. I'll roll her fingers to get some prints. You haven't been printed before, have you, ma'am?"

"Me? Ach, no. Never. Not even a drivin' infraction. Well, no. That's not exactly true. One time, when I was waitin' for me Jimmy, God rest his soul, I didn't see the sign, and I turned up a wrong way street—"

"Can you point out any surfaces you may have touched, Mrs. O'Shea?" Detective Gill interrupted.

"Yes. I mean, no. I didn't touch anythin'. Me Michael is always tellin' me about—"

"O'Shea? You're Mike O'Shea's mom?" the forensics officer said.

"Yes. Do ye know him?"

"No, but I've heard an awful lot about him. And you. Amanda Black wouldn't stop talking about both of you at the last crime scene we were at together. Said it was you who practically solved one of her cases."

"Yes, well, I just made a few suggestions to me Michael. It was Mandy," the two officers looked at one another and smiled, "who did all the work to find the madman involved in that one. I only suggested a few points of law..."

Mary-Margaret let her words trail off, noticing that Detective Gill's eyebrow was unnaturally raised.

"Truth to be told," she added, "I'm not all that heartbroken. It's not like she was me sister, Detective. As I said, I hardly knew her."

"It doesn't seem that many people did. Not even her daughter. Here's my card. If you think of anything, just give me a call," Detective Gill said, leading

Mary-Margaret back out to the street. "I've also heard that Detective Black thinks quite highly of you."

"Well, that's very kind of—"

"And I've also heard that you have a tendency to meddle."

Mary-Margaret stopped short, the thought of invoking that pox crossing her mind for the briefest of seconds.

"This is a homicide. Very serious business. It's all fun and games until someone gets hurt or evidence gets lost. The last thing I need is someone who thinks she's an amateur sleuth poking her nose around."

"If ye are referrin' to me, Detective, ye have no worries there. I've got me hands full with the church fall bazaar and taking care of me Michael and Sally-next-door's dog and—"

"Excellent. Would you like one of my officers to give you a ride home?" Detective Gill offered, looking at the uniformed men.

That's all me Michael would need to see now. Me gettin' out of a police cruiser. She waved off the offer.

"Suit yourself. But you might want to come clean about your foot." He turned back to return to the crime scene.

This web is gettin' tangled, Mary-Margaret thought as she walked towards the bus stop. I best get those crutches back. Me Michael will be askin' a few hard questions if he sees me skippin' about like this.

"Mary-Margaret!" a woman's voice called out from a car that was stopped a few feet in front of her.

"Oh, Chrystal. I was just on me way home."

"Where's your car?" Chrystal asked, looking along the street.

"Took transit."

"Hop in. I'll give you a ride." She reached across the front seat to open the passenger door.

"Are ye sure it's not too much trouble?"

"Not at all. And I'd like to talk to you. About the investigation."

Chapter Thirteen

"They're having a candlelight vigil tonight at the co-op for Mom. Will you come? It would mean a lot to me."

"Knew nothin' about it, but now that I do, of course. I'm at me Michael's these days. A bit of a drive, luv, but I'll direct ye as we go."

"How well do you know this Detective Gill?" Chrystal asked.

"I know him about as well as ye do. Why?"

"I don't like him."

"Ye don't have to, now do ye? I mean, as long as he finds out what happened to yer mam."

"I know what happened to my mother. She was murdered."

"Ye know what I mean, luv."

"I don't think he's taking her murder seriously."

"Ach, I know what ye are sayin', luv, but he's all we've got, or so they say. We've barely just begun—"

"He seems to think that I may have something to do with my mother's death."

"Oh. And why is that?"

"He seems to think that, because I'm her sole beneficiary, I have a motive to kill her."

"Well, if ye put it like that, I think ye have a motive to kill her as well, although—"

Chrystal looked sharply over at Mary-Margaret.

"Have you seen where she lives? Do you think she has any money? Like she's got some great fortune stashed away?" Chrystal said, her voice getting shrill. She stopped, took a deep breath, and continued. "I'm sorry, but, like I told Detective Gill, her death is probably going to cost me money once I pay for her burial, the cost of clearing her apartment and getting rid of her stuff, and whatever debts she may have. And I know she has debts—that last boyfriend took her for everything she had and more. No, I think Detective Gill could rule me out pretty quickly."

"So what about this last boyfriend?"

"Gone with the wind."

"And we know this how?"

"The last Mom heard from him was when he sent her a postcard from Florida."

"He could have come back and—"

"You're serious, aren't you?" Chrystal said, again looking over at Mary-Margaret.

"'Tis possible."

"No. He took everything she had. That gorgeous condo? He had her sign half of it over to him. This was all just after I'd caught up with her again. If I'd been around, none of this would have happened. There's no reason he'd want to kill my mother. She was already dead to him."

The car sped up.

"I could see that he was a con artist the moment I set eyes on him. He had that look, you know? And I think he knew that I saw right through him, which is why he exited stage right pretty quickly after I came along."

"So he's out. Yer not a suspect, in my opinion, so that leaves who?"

"That's what I was hoping Detective Gill would tell me, but apparently, even though I'm *the deceased's* daughter, I don't need to know anything."

"Perhaps I can help ye out a bit there. As ye know, me son, Michael, is a detective, and he tells me all sorts of things at the dining room table about how he investigates—"

"That's what I wanted to talk to you about," Chrystal interrupted as she turned a corner. "Word on the street is that you have quite a reputation with the homicide squad."

"Do I now?"

"Mary-Margaret, would you investigate my mother's murder?"

Mary-Margaret's eyes widened.

"I know you'll find the killer before he does."

"Well now, that's quite a vote of confidence for me."

"I'll pay you."

"Absolutely not. Me Michael would have me hide if he knew I was takin' money to solve murders."

"So you'll do it for free then?"

"Listen, luv, I'm dead chuffed that ye think I could manage such a thing, and I know I could, but there's a lot to an investigation that I don't have access to."

"Like what? You saw the crime scene, you saw the body at the morgue, you can talk to people at the co-op as well as the police can. Will you do this for me? For my mother?"

"Ach, luv, if I do take this on, and I'm not saying that I will, I can't make any promises. I mean, I do know Frank at the morgue, and I can always call our Mandy if me Michael won't help, but I'm thinkin' that it's just too fresh in yer mind now and ye need to give Billy Gilly's lads a moment to find their feet before ye start calling in the likes of—"

"You? Why?"

The car was moving a bit faster than Mary-Margaert thought was prudent, given the number of children on the sidewalks.

"Well, I've also got a lot on me plate at the moment," Mary-Margaret said, almost as quickly as the car was going.

"I need you. If you wait, the leads will go cold. And someone else could be murdered."

"That last bit is a wee stretch, luv. And ye do know that there's a speed limit on the roadway here, I'm sure."

"Is it a stretch?" Chrystal asked, slowing down. "How do we know that whoever killed my mother didn't already kill someone else?"

"Luv, these are questions that ye need to be asking Detective Gill. He's yer man. And he's got more resources at his disposal than—"

"I don't like the way he talks to me."

"If ye are referrin' to the other day," Mary-Margaret began, not wanting to use the word 'morgue', "I'm all for agreein' that he may not have been at his best."

"And hasn't been since. I've gone in for questioning, and he grilled me about my relationship with my mother. As if I could have killed her."

"Well, I think we've already been over that."

"I've given him photos and old address books, and everything I could think of that was tied to Mom," Chrystal said. "Why would I do that if I was the killer?"

"It is a police investigation and all. I'm sure he'll sort ye out. I mean, we're all suspects, although ye do have a bit more of a motive than, say, the lad that has already taken everythin' yer mam had to take or some random madman."

Chyrstal kept her eyes on the road.

"Maybe I could ask around," Mary-Margaret finally said.

"My mother had just started seeing someone," Chrystal said, stopping the car at the stop sign.

"So I heard."

"Really?" Chrystal said, looking over at her passenger.

"From Nancy, the super."

"Did she tell you his name?"

"Jerry."

"Yes. That's it. Jerry. Jerry LaMarshe," Chrystal said. "He's seventeen years younger than she is...was."

"Well done, Jane Ann!" Mary-Margaret shouted, then realizing that she was talking about someone her driver apparently disapproved of, added in a small voice, "Sorry, luv."

"Has a Mini Cooper. Cops impounded it," Chrystal added, her foot getting heavier on the accelerator.

"Oh."

"They've already had Jerry in for questioning."

"And ye know all of this because how?"

"One of the cops at my mom's place told me." The car slowed as the green light turned to yellow and then stopped as the traffic lights turned red.

"And why would he be tellin' ye that?"

"He also told me that they've ruled out Jerry as a suspect."

"Well, that somethin'. Do ye think this lad that told ye knew all of this, or just thought he knew?"

"Until I hear otherwise, I'm going to believe it. What I really want to know, though, is why they still have Jerry's car if he's not a suspect?"

"Well, from all the stories me Michael's told, I'm wonderin' if there wasn't somethin' that came up in the questionin' about yer mam that led to somethin' else." *Or this lad is leadin' ye on.*

Chrystal stared at her friend for a moment before a horn honked behind them.

"The light," Mary-Margaret pointed out. "It's green now, luv. The car in front of us—"

"Oh. Right," Chrystal replied, waving her hand as she looked in her rearview mirror at the driver behind her before setting the car in motion again.

"D'ye think it might be best if we chatted about this later?"

"No, I'm fine."

"I see. What do we know about this Jerry lad?"

Chrystal sighed.

"That bad, is it?"

"I think he was just one of Mom's...diversions."

"Come again?" Mary-Margaret said, looking over at Chrystal.

"Well, there isn't...wasn't...isn't... much to him, you know? I mean, yes, he is—was— much younger than she is—was, but that was about it."

"Did he work? Have a job? Friends? Family?"

"I'm not sure," Chrystal said. "I think so. I think Mom said he worked in some factory."

"Honest work," Mary-Margaret commented. "Left here at the lights, luv."

"I guess, but hardly what I would have thought Mom would look for in a man."

"And what did ye think she was lookin' for in a man? Ye can go, now. The light has turned yellow."

"Oh. Right," Chrystal said, making the turn slowly before continuing. "I don't know what she was looking for. The usual, I guess. Steady. Kind. Smart."

"Is that what she was lookin' for, or is that what ye are lookin' for? And what's to say this Jerry lad wasn't all that, even though he worked in a factory?" Mary-Margaret said, accentuating the last few words, thinking of her Jimmy, the factory worker.

"I know. It sounds horrible, but I always pictured her with someone—"

"And there's yer problem. Ye always pictured her, yet ye hardly knew her."

The car glided to a stop as the lights at the intersection turned red. The two sat silently as cars passed in front of them.

"Green, luv. The light is green."

"Oh. Right."

"Had you met him?" Mary-Margaret asked.

"Yes."

"And?"

"He had very clean hands."

"Very clean hands?"

"Yes. You know. For someone who's supposed to be a factory worker."

"Well, not everyone who works in a factory works on the machines."

"I just...I don't know. I guess he was alright. I mean, yes, he was steady, he had a job—"

"Right here!" Mary-Margaret interrupted.

"And he seemed to make Mom happy," Chrystal concluded as she completed the turn.

"So, wherein lies the problem?"

"I just thought she could do better."

"What's better than someone who makes ye happy?" Mary-Margaret said, almost to herself.

"Well, Mom didn't seem to have a hard time finding men who made her happy," Chrystal shot back with surprising sharpness.

"Happy and amused are two very different things. And turn left here. At the stop sign."

69

"When your standards are lowered…."

Mary-Margaret looked quickly over to Chrystal before looking back at the road in front of her.

"After finding her, I realized that my mom was this party girl who was past her prime. When I was little," Chrystal said, rolling through the stop sign as she turned onto a busy road, "she always seemed so smart and stylish and fun. And then she left. And then…."

"And then ye grew up, luv. And yer mam grew up, too. Became her own person. Hard as it may seem to grasp, even me own children began to see their mam as human at one point, full of flaws and imperfections. We can't hold up our ends forever, although, I must say, I do believe I've managed quite well, all things considered."

"But I wanted her to be *that* mom," Chrystal said, tears beginning to run down her cheeks. "And she could have become that mom."

"No, luv. She couldn't," Mary-Margaret said, wishing she had some tissues with her before taking a deep breath, "Now, where might I find our Jerry?"

"Why? They've ruled him out," Chrystal said, wiping the tears off of her face with her sleeve and then taking a deep breath in to capture any snot that might have begun to flow from her nose.

"But they still have his car, didn't ye say?"

"Yes. So they still think he did it?"

"Not necessarily. Now, mind yerself here, luv. The traffic gets a bit much. He might be involved in somethin' else,"

"So why wouldn't Gill just say that?" Chrystal said, ignoring Mary-Margaret's warning.

"That Jerry is involved in something else?"

"I don't know. Perhaps he thought it wasn't of yer concern."

"My mother has been murdered. Don't you think everything related to her would be my concern?"

"Not if it had nothin' to do with yer mam's death, no."

"What else could Jerry be involved in?"

"We have no way of knowin', do we luv? I can do some askin' around but I can't promise anythin'."

"So you'll take the case?"

"No, I'll ask about the car."

"But you'll talk to Jerry?" Chrystal looked over at Mary-Margaret.

"Well, yes. If only to satisfy me own curiosity. Do ye know where I might find him?"

"I think Mom said it was—yes, it was, because he was always bringing over cookies and things. He works at the cookie factory in the west end down by the lake."

"So not too far from the church, then?"

"No, actually."

"Or the co-op."

"No. Just around the corner, come to think of it."

"Right at the lights up the road, luv," Mary-Margaret said, pointing to the traffic lights a couple of blocks ahead of them. "Yes. I'll have a wee word with this Jerry lad, and we'll go from there. Is there anyone else yer man might have known?"

"There's Mom's next-door neighbor," Chrystal said. "She'd mentioned him a couple of times."

"As a...?"

"Friend."

"At least she had some discernment when it came to the lads," Mary-Margaret said. "Wouldn't want to be snugglin' up to that one, that's for sure. A right up ahead, and we're onto me Michael's street, luv."

Chrystal turned the corner. "This is me house—me Michael's house—coming up on the left. Ye can just let me off here."

"When will you get back to me about Jerry and the neighbor?" Chrystal asked.

"Ye don't ask much, do ye, luv? Give me a day or two, and we'll see what we have."

Mary-Margaret thanked Chrystal for the ride and got out of the car.

"You're welcome. See you tonight. And thanks for taking on the case," Chrystal shouted as she drove off.

"I have not taken on the case!" Mary-Margaret hollered after the car.

"Mom?" Michael called out from the front door.

"Michael. Ye are home."

"Who are you yelling at, and what are you saying?"

"It matters not now, Michael. Come down and give yer mam an arm. Me foot is throbbin'. I left me crutches at the church, and I've been—"

"Your crutches are here, Mom. Arthur brought them over. Said something about having to get a car out of the pound...?"

"Yes, of course," Mary-Margaret said, grabbing hold of her son's arm.

"Do tell," Michael said drily, helping his mother inside the house.

"Can ye just put on the kettle, luv? The logic behind it is too complicated for me mind to unravel before I have a good strong cuppa."

"I'm sure."

"But before ye go, luv, can you be a superstar and find me a pen and some paper? I've got a few things needin' scribblin' before me mind goes blank."

Chapter Fourteen

"Ta, luv," Mary-Margaret said, taking the cup of tea from Michael. "And a wee biscuit?"

"Right." Michael rolled his eyes as he turned back to the kitchen.

"I'll not be burdenin' ye much longer, Michael. Doctor says I'm makin' a miraculous recovery."

"When did you have time to go see the doctor?" Michael asked, returning and holding the box of cookies out to his mother.

"Ach, Michael. This is no way to serve biscuits! Take them back and bring them on a plate. Ye know better."

Michael took the box of cookies back to the kitchen, returning with six on a plate.

"Now that's better, me son."

"So the doctor was saying?"

"Oh, yes. Me doctor. Says I'm almost right as rain. Don't even need the crutches, in fact."

"You better tell Arthur that. He seemed quite certain you'd need them. And your foot seemed pretty tender a few minutes ago."

"That was just me needin' some steadyin'. Haven't eaten all day, ye know. Not good for me blood sugar. And wantin' to give me big strong son a squeeze, of course."

"I didn't know you had a blood sugar issue."

"I don't. No more than the next, which is to say we all get a little wobbly on our pins sometimes. Can ye put another splash of milk in me tea, luv? It's a bit sharp for me likin'. Are ye sure ye used the Barry's I brought over?

Of course, I'd get up and get it meself, but as ye have noted, I'm a bit wobbly at the moment."

Michael dutifully took the mug of tea back to the kitchen.

I can't keep this foot business up much longer, Mary-Margaret thought. Less said, easier mended, and too much may have been said already.

And then Michael was back.

"Ach, luv. Perfect. Just like ye."

The cell phone in Mary-Margaret's purse began to ring.

"Hello? Yes. Yes. Hold on a minute, will ye, luv?" She looked over at Michael. "Would ye mind? Personal call. I'd go off to me room meself if—"

Michael started up the stairs without listening to the rest of what his mother might have to say.

"I should likely not be tellin' ye this, but I know ye have a keen interest," Frank said, his voice lowered to a whisper.

"I'm all ears."

"We've just finished up the autopsy on yer girl. Stabbed to death. They're saying fourteen times. With somethin' that wasn't so very sharp. Likely just a regular dinner knife. Stabber was likely left-handed, although they're plannin' on keeping that information from the media. 'Hold back,' they call it. Somethin' only they and the murderer would know. Can't talk now, but I just wanted to let ye know. Any chance of dinner with ye tonight?"

"Brill, Francis, simply brill. I can't do dinner this eve. Nor tomorrow. How is Saturday lookin'?"

"Grand. I'll see ye at O'Leary's then. Say around seven?"

"With bells on. And thanks for this."

"No one can know, yeah?"

"Me lips are sealed."

As soon as she hung up, Mary-Margaret pressed auto-dial.

"Arthur, 'tis me, luv. Can ye come 'round in a few and take me to the co-op? There's going to be a vigil for Jane Ann, and I need to be there. Ye know, it's not uncommon for the murderer to show up at things like this. Get a sense of what emotional carnage they've caused and all."

"I'm on it. But how am I supposed to pick you up?"

"Daphne. She's parked in me drive. Keys are in the kitchen in the second cookie jar on the counter, where ye never clean. Let yerself in with the key I gave ye, and I'll see ye here in fifteen minutes."

"You want me to drive Daphne?"

"Absolutely not!" Mary-Margaret was horrified at the thought. Daphne was Mary-Margaret's eggshell-blue 1964 Renault Dauphine and her pride and joy. "Which is to say, yes, I need ye to bring the car here, and then no, I only just want ye to look like ye are drivin' me car in the event that me Michael happens to look out back as I'm comin' or goin'."

She hung up just as Michael came back down the stairs.

"Too soon?" he asked, smiling at her as he walked towards the kitchen.

"Come again?"

"You're up to something, aren't you, Mom."

"Me? Not at all. Just waitin' for Arthur to pop by. We're going out for a bit."

"You and Arthur? Where?"

"What are ye, a policeman?"

"Seriously, Mom—"

"I'm off to the vigil for Jane Ann, if ye must know."

"With Arthur."

"With Arthur. Just in case I need a strong arm to hold me up." She looked pointedly at her foot.

"How are you getting there?"

"Arthur's bringing Daphne 'round."

"You're letting him drive your car? No one drives your car. But the more I know, the less I want to know," Michael said, shaking his head as he rummaged through the cupboards for something to snack on.

"There are a few pots and pans in the sink that ye've likely seen but paid no heed to, luv. Can ye give them a scrub while yer in there? I'd hop up do it meself, but, what with me foot and all...."

Ten minutes later, Mary-Margaret's cell phone rang.

"MM, I'm here in the laneway."

"I'll be right out."

"Mom, Arthur's here. Either that or there's a bag lady sitting in your car," Michael said, walking back through the living room with a plate of cookies.

"Ach. Ye won't get a plate for yer mam, but ye load one up when it's biscuits for yerself. I see how this wheel's turnin'. Well, I'm off, then."

"What in the name of—" Mary-Margaret began.

"Get in before anyone sees us!" Arthur whispered loudly as he hopped out of the driver's seat and ran around to the passenger's side.

"Ye don't have to tell me twice," she said. Arthur got in and looked first for the non-existent side view mirror before adjusting the rearview mirror to face himself. "Not as good a job as I would have liked, but you didn't give me much notice."

"Notice of what?" Mary-Margaret asked, looking over at Arthur. She wasn't sure if it was the ratty long gray wig Arthur had perched on his head, the smock-like overcoat that appeared to cover an equally smock-like dress, or the huge black old-lady lace-up shoes that she found to be the most unusual. Glancing quickly at her wristwatch, she returned the mirror to its original position, released the parking brake, and backed out of the tiny parking spot into the alley behind Michael's house. "How did ye—"

"Years of cosplay have allowed me to become very good at costumes and makeup," Arthur explained. "Now, you are probably wondering why I'm dressed up, looking as old as you."

"As old as me?" Mary-Margaret shrieked as she drove the car out onto the main street. "I don't think—"

"I know. Brilliant, isn't it? Who would suspect another old woman at a memorial service? But we don't have time to get into how I managed to pull this off. Here's my plan. You go into the vigil and do your thing. I'll hang back in the car for a few minutes so people don't think we're together, and then I'll emerge and make my way into the crowd."

"But—"

"I know. Genius. While you're mourning and crying and all of that, I'll be taking pictures of the crowd."

"And with what, pray tell," Mary-Margaret asked, taking her eyes off the road ahead momentarily to get another look at Arthur, "shall ye be takin' photos with?"

"With this hatpin camera." Arthur pulled a pillbox hat out from inside his coat.

Mary-Margaret shook her head.

"Here's the plan," Arthur said, pulling the rearview mirror towards himself again as he repositioned the wig on his head. "You mingle. I gather intel."

Mary-Margaret impatiently pulled the rearview mirror back into position.

"Arthur, luv, ye are makin' me head spin like a shiny penny in a poor man's hand."

"Trust me, MM."

"Ye are not the first lad who's said that to me with disastrous outcomes, luv."

After several minutes of silence—likely the longest period of silence between the two—they arrived. Mary-Margaret pulled the car over to the curb near the co-op. Arthur tried, in vain, to conceal his large frame below the dashboard of the tiny car,

"The only downside—"

"The only?"

"Yes. The only downside to my plan is that I didn't have time to figure out an inconspicuous way to take pictures with this camera."

"Yer jokin'," Mary-Margaret said with a laugh. "So ye have gone to all of this trouble for naught? Sometimes I honestly think—and don't take this the wrong way, luv—that the wheel is spinnin' up there in yer head but the hamster's dead."

"I am not joking, MM. Fear not, however. I have a workaround."

"I am on tenterhooks."

"I've cleverly installed the camera into the hat so that with a gentle tap on the side of it, a picture is taken."

"So what I'm hearin' is that ye'll be wanderin' around whackin' yerself on the noggin' for the duration?"

"I suppose," Arthur conceded.

"Give me strength," Mary-Margaret sighed as she pulled the parking brake up, knocking Arthur in the head.

"Ouch!" he cried out, rubbing his forehead as he popped up from his crouched position.

"We're off to a right grand start, then." Mary-Margaret looked over at Arthur, blinked a couple of times, and then redirected her attention to opening her door safely. "Be sure to lock the car on yer side when ye get out."

Chapter Fifteen

Mary-Margaret had never actually been to a vigil before, but she quickly decided that it was like a wake without the alcohol. She saw Monique Prudhomme, Irene Ashford, and a few other people from the church amongst the forty or so people standing outside of the co-op on the lawn. Most were clustered into small groups, some of whom were laughing while others were talking in hushed tones. She wondered if Mr. Fisher was amongst them. Jane Ann had, after all, considered him a friend.

"Mary-Margaret?" a voice called out.

"Yes, Mr. Gill," she replied, recognizing him immediately more by the way he stood out from the casually dressed crowd in his finely tailored suit and shined shoes than by actual memory.

"That's Detective Gill. What brings you here this evening?"

"Well, the same thing that brings us all out, I suppose. Just payin' me respects to me friend, Jane Ann."

"Have you been speaking with Chrystal?" he continued, standing closer to her than she would have preferred.

"And if I have, Mr. Gill? There's no crime in that, is there?" She did not look at him, but she refused to take a step back from him.

"No," he admitted, his lips tightening to a thin line. "But there is a crime in interfering with police investigation."

"As I am well aware. Me son, Michael, is a police detective, as I believe I've mentioned before."

"Yes, you have. So I'm expecting that you, of all people, will respect the investigative process, and while I can appreciate that you mean well, that you will keep your distance."

"*Mean well?* Is that what ye said, Mr. Gill? Mean well?" Mary-Margaret turned and looked the homicide investigator up and down. "I do not mean well. I was an acquaintance, no, a sister-parishioner, of your deceased. I have also been asked by her own daughter to—"

"I can appreciate that you mean well," Detective Gill repeated, "and I can also appreciate that you have a keen sense of the importance of maintaining the integrity of a homicide investigation, your son being a police detective and all...."

"Are ye patronizin' me, Mr. Gill?"

"No, I'm cautioning you. Not only are we investigating a murder, we are looking for a murderer. Which means that there is someone out there who has killed before. We don't want him to kill again, and we certainly don't want anything to happen to you, do we, Mrs. O'Shea?"

"Did ye speak to her ex-boyfriend?"

"Pardon me?"

"The ex. The one before the current. Don't tell me yer hat rack has been involved in one too many dustups as well? She broke his heart, did our Jane Ann, and he broke her bank."

"I'm sure she did, not unlike many other hearts, so I'm learning."

"And what of him runnin' off with all of her money?"

"I assure you that a thorough investi—"

"Well, we all know 'tis the closest male relative that's likely the murderer."

"Thank you for the tip, Mrs. O'Shea. I'll have to make sure that nugget of investigative gold gets into the Homicide Investigator's Handbook. This may surprise you, but this is not my first criminal investigation."

"I wasn't goin' to be the one to say it, but...."

The two faced each other like a couple of cats in a dark alley.

"If ye don't mind, *Detective* Gill," Mary-Margaret said after a few moments of prickly silence, "I'd like to join in the vigil. Now excuse me."

"I'll be calling your son to make sure you've understood," Gill called after her.

"I'll be ringing Mandy to have a word about ye as well," she muttered under her breath to no one in particular.

* * *

Having adjusted himself to his satisfaction, Arthur exited Daphne and walked toward the crowd, tapping the side of his hat and wishing he had opted for a less restricting pair of shoes for the occasion.

"This is a horrible, horrible tragedy, wouldn't you say?" he said in a high falsetto voice to a young woman standing on the periphery of the crowd.

"I guess," the woman replied with indifference, trying not to stare at the huge woman standing beside her.

"Did you know the deceased?" Arthur continued, his voice cracking as he tried to keep the pitch high. "The murdered woman?"

"No," the woman said, moving away from Arthur. "My friend lives here. I just came to see him tonight. Had no idea this was happening."

"Just as well, I suppose," Arthur continued, scanning the crowd and tapping his hat.

"I guess." She quickly walked into the middle of the gathering without looking back.

"Indeed," Arthur said, his voice dropping to its usual tone as he scanned the crowd, all the while tapping the side of his hat.

* * *

"Attention, everyone," a woman Mary-Margaret recognized as Nancy, the building superintendent, said, jumping as the feedback from her microphone squawked. A young man raced over to the amplifier and turned the volume down. "Thanks, Raul. Never was good at this sort of thing."

She turned back to the crowd and smiled and then put on her most somber face.

"As you know, we are here again, this time to remember our dear friend and neighbor, Jane Ann Hill."

A loud wail came from someone in the crowd. Everyone turned toward the source.

"Don't mind me, lads," Arthur said, resuming his falsetto voice. "'Tis sadder than an Irish rain on a young bride's weddin', is this!"

He broke down into a series of sobs.

"Oh, for the love of God," Mary-Margaret muttered under her breath.

"Carry on, me lovelies," Arthur called out, his head buried in his hands. "I'll be fine. We'll all be fine. Except for Jane Ann, of course."

The wailing got louder before a group of women gathered around Arthur and began rubbing his back and neck.

"The hat! The hat! Don't touch the hat!" Arthur cried out in his real voice as he felt his wig being pushed off his head.

"Excuse me, everyone," Mary-Margaret said, making her way to Arthur. "Me...sister...is very...emotional. Just let her alone now, and we'll be on our way."

She grabbed Arthur firmly by the arm and frog-marched him out of the crowd towards her car.

"For the love of Dymphna, lad! What was that all about?" she demanded as soon as they were out of earshot of the others.

"I was just playing—"

"The fool is what ye were playin'. And I thought ye were just goin' to watch the crowds, not be the center of attention." She finally let go of his arm to rummage through her purse for her car keys, not slowing her steps in the least.

"How was I supposed to know that no one else would be crying, MM?" Arthur asked plaintively, almost running in his high heels to keep up with her, wincing at the pain hammering his feet with every step.

"I'm sure there were other moist eyes, lad, but ye were the only one wailin' like a banshee."

Arthur stopped and bent down to take off one and then the other ill-fitting shoe, leaving them where they lay, before scurrying to catch up with Mary-Margaret.

"Anyway," he said, "I think I got a pic of everyone. I'll download the files when I get home, and then we can start ID'ing them all, and then—"

"Let's just get ourselves out of this mess before we start into another, shall we?" Mary-Margaret interrupted, unlocking the door to the driver's side before hopping in and reaching over to unlock the passenger door.

"Gold," Arthur exclaimed, pulling the wig off his head before detaching the pillbox hat and pulling the tiny camera off, stuffing the latter into his pocket.

Chapter Sixteen

F ridays were a welcome time for Mary-Margaret, not just because
they used to signify the end of a five-day stretch doing anything and
everything at the church, but because it meant a night at O'Leary's
with her dear friends, Eleanor and Angus Corrigan.

"Well, come in," Eleanor called to her friend as Angus stood up. Like the
O'Sheas, the Corrigans had emigrated to the U.S. as a young couple with
children who had arrived like a steep set of stairs, resulting in the two families
becoming fast friends. When Jimmy died, it was Eleanor who made sure the
O'Shea children were dressed and ready for the funeral, and it was Eleanor
who put Mary-Margaret's name forward when the opening for a secretary
came up at the church. And it was Angus who made sure that Mary-Margaret
got all that was coming to her by way of pensions and insurance money.

"Ach, sorry I'm late, me luvs. It's been quite the week," Mary-Margaret
exhaled, dropping down onto the wooden chair Angus had pulled out for
her.

The regular server placed a half pint of the crown float in front of Mary-
Margaret.

"Nectar of the gods. Forgive me for using Yer name in vain. Slainte." She
took a large sip from her glass. Eleanor and Angus raised their wine glasses
in response, taking much more refined sips.

"Is everything all right, then, dear?" Angus asked.

"Well, let me tell ye, I've had the most unusual week yet at the church,"
Mary-Margaret began, taking another sip of her drink before filling her
friends in on her activities.

"I wouldn't go nosing about in something like that," Angus cautioned, nodding to the server as she placed their plates of fish and chips down in front of them.

"And why not, Angus?" Eleanor countered. "She could be one of those private investigator types, like something you read in those paperbacks you pick up at the airport. What harm can come of it versus the good she might be able to do?"

She nodded approvingly at Mary-Margaret, who was more like a sister to her than a friend.

"I don't like it, Eleanor," Angus said with a huff. "Let the police handle it. You never know what people are about these days, and I don't think you're the one to figure it out."

"Well, her Michael might be able to do something—" Eleanor began.

"And I'm sure she's asked, haven't you, and I'm sure he's told you the same thing as I've done. We're not getting any younger, Mary-Margaret, and given that there's foul play involved—"

"Are ye callin' me old, Angus Corrigan?"

"I'm not saying anything of the sort. I'm just saying—"

"I don't see the harm in having a second set of eyes look at it, Angus," Eleanor said.

"And I'm sure the police have had many eyes on this situation."

"That ham-fisted flatfoot they've got leadin' this investigation? Horrible man, is he. No compassion whatsoever. Practically threatened me at Jane Ann's vigil. Speakin' of which—it's an odd thing, these vigils. Not a dram of whisky in sight."

"A police detective threatened you?" Eleanor gasped.

"Indeed. A homicide detective, no less. Told me to keep me distance or he'd—"

"I agree with him. I think you're getting very close to meddling in legal business," Angus admonished.

Eleanor gave her husband a steely glance before looking down at the battered fish she had barely touched. She began pushing it around on her plate with her fork.

"Perhaps we've all had a long week," Mary-Margaret finally said. "And here's me shootin' off at the gob with not a thought in me brain about anyone else. Angus, would ye mind catchin' our girl's eye for a wee splash of vinegar? The fish seems a bit dry tonight. Do ye find it dry, Eleanor?"

"I suppose I do," Eleanor replied, looking down at the mess she had made of her plate. "Perhaps another glass of wine would help. You're both driving, so you're cut off, but I'll take the plunge and have another."

And with that, the tension dissipated, and the evening continued on as it usually did, with a few laughs, some clever insights into the events of the day, and a fair bit of gossip.

"Now remember, Mary-Margaret," Angus cautioned as they were leaving the pub, "leave this detective work to the real detect—"

"Oi!" Mary-Margaret yelled out at the figure, fumbling with something in his hand near the driver's side of her car.

The young man stood perfectly still for a moment and then shoved whatever was in his hand into his pocket before running from the parking lot onto the street. Dodging a couple of cars, he looked back once and was gone. Mary-Margaret began a hurried walk towards her car. Eleanor looked at Angus, who then began to trot after Mary-Margaret.

"Did he get in? Did he get anything?" Angus called to her, winded after only a few short steps.

Using the flashlight from her cell phone, Mary-Margaret did a quick scan of the car's exterior as she raced around it, trying the door handles as she went.

"No, thanks be to St. Frances of Rome," Mary-Margaret said just before she caught a glimmer of something on the ground by her feet, where the man had been standing.

"Don't pick it up, Mary-Margaret," Angus said, seeing her reaching down. "It could be a clue."

"Indeed. It could be," she said, picking up and then opening the wallet. "Not a wealthy man, is our..." she pulled a library card from the slim plastic wallet, "Robert Jackson."

"I think you should call the police," Eleanor said.

"And say what? That she's got a wallet with what—a bus pass, a couple of bucks, and a library card in it?" Angus chuckled. "Not even a credit card worth reporting."

"That she's got the ID of someone who was trying to break into her car," Eleanor corrected.

"I know what I'll do," Mary-Margaret said, looking closer at the library card before pocketing it and tossing the shiny wallet back onto the pavement. "I'll call me Michael. He'll know who this lad is and have a wee word with him."

"If Michael is not interested in helping you with a murder investigation, what makes you think he'll be interested in this?" Angus said.

"Because I am his mam, and this involves me directly. If me Michael won't, perhaps I'll have a wee word with this lad meself."

Mary-Margert got into her old car, turned on the engine, and, with a wave out the window, drove out of the parking lot, getting lost in the red taillights of the Friday night traffic.

Chapter Seventeen

"I'm off, then, me son," Mary-Margaret announced to Michael as she reached for the back door.

"Was it you or Arthur who was driving on Thursday night?"

"And ye are askin' me this now, two days later, because...?"

"Because I haven't seen you since then, and your car is in my parking spot, and I've been parking on the street and getting parking tickets the last two days."

"Don't they know that ye are the police? Why are ye gettin' ticketed?"

"It doesn't work that way, Mom."

"So whether 'twas me or Arthur drivin', ye would still be gettin' the tickets."

"But if it was you, how did you manage that with your broken—"

"Well, as ye know, I can't tell a lie, Michael. I was not. 'Twas Arthur."

"So then why wouldn't he take the car back to your place after dropping you off?"

"Because I needed the car to go to O'Leary's last night. Ach," Mary-Margaret continued, before Michael could get a word in, "he's a disaster waitin' to happen behind the wheel, is that one! Lovely lad, but honestly. And he shouldn't be drivin' regardless. Doesn't even have a..." Mary-Margaret stopped herself from finishing the sentence.

"You drove your car to O'Leary's?"

"Well, 'tis not like I had more than half a pint, if that's what yer on about."

"No, I'm on about your broken ankle. Your right ankle, isn't it?"

"Foot. Right foot, yes. And it's healin'."

"Right foot. But still broken with an...invisible cast?"

"Exactly."

"And where are your crutches?"

Mary-Margert froze for a second, then looked first towards her right and then towards her left underarm.

"Are they invisible, too?"

"Ach, Michael. Ye are talkin' foolishness now. I'm five minutes late for a ten-minute drive, so while I'd love to explain meself—not that I have to—the logic behind it is too complicated for me mind to unravel to ye in this moment, so I'll be on me way." She walked out, adding as she turned to close the back door behind her, "Regardin' those parkin' tickets, I'll pay them, although ye ought to look into a street parkin' pass for yer car goin' forward. Ta ra!"

* * *

"Lovely to see you, Mary-Margaret," Laura-Jean McQueen said, directing a group of young men to move a large table into the middle of the cordoned-off parking lot.

"And where else on God's green earth would I be this mornin'?" Mary-Margaret asked. "That doesn't go there, lads! Put it over there, beside the church. If ye set it there, whoever is sellin' the raffle tickets will be a puddle on the asphalt by noon."

"No," Laura-Jean corrected. "Over there, please. We're not selling raffle tickets this time, Mary-Margaret. We're going to charge for parking instead. By the entrance there, fellas. Thanks!"

"Paid parking? At a church bazaar? With no raffle? Jesus, Mary, and Joseph!" Mary-Margaret crossed herself. "Does Father Miguel know about this?"

"It was his idea," Laura-Jean said, smiling towards the window of Father Miguel's office. "Is there anything in particular you're looking to buy, Mary-Margaret? Perhaps one of the Catholic Women's League ladies can help you find it?"

"Lookin' to buy? I am not lookin' to buy anythin'. I am lookin' to run the church bazaar that I have overseen since before yer head stopped runnin' on all cylinders!"

"Ah, Mary-Margaret." Father Miguel said as he walked up to the two women. "I see your car in the parking lot. You drove it, I'm assuming. So your foot has healed?"

"Me foot is just fine, thank ye for askin'. 'Tis a miracle of nature, to be sure. And so, if ye don't mind, ye can have Laura-Jean McQueen step down from her high and mighty post so that I can get the bazaar organized before the people start arrivin'."

"I'm afraid that won't be necessary, Mary-Margaret. Laura-Jean has things well in order. If you do want to help out, you could start by moving your car. Unless you want to give Laura-Jean the five dollars we're charging to park there."

Mary-Margaret's jaw dropped.

"Father, a word, please?" one of the men setting up the games section interrupted.

"Certainly. Now, if you'll excuse me, Mary-Margaret. And if you need help moving your car..."

"Mary-Margaret!" a woman called out.

Mary-Margaret turned and saw Chrystal Hill.

"What is it, me lamb?" she called back, giving Laura-Jean an icy glare before rushing towards Chrystal.

"I am so sorry to come here today while you're so busy with the bazaar, but there's no one else to turn to, and I need your help."

"There's no one else to turn to, and ye need my help?" Mary-Margaret repeated loud enough for Laura-Jean, Father Miguel, and anyone within earshot to hear. "Of course. What is it?"

"The police said they'll be done with my mother's apartment later this afternoon, and I really want to get in there to clean it up and get her things out. But I'm afraid to go alone."

"Well, luv, I'm not much for the cleanin', ever since me Michael introduced me to Arthur through the agency, but I'll gladly come in to have a look 'round and help ye with the sortin', if need be. Thanks to The New Girl, I've had a lot of experience sortin' these last few days."

"Mary-Margaret would never let anything like this happen!" Monique Prudhomme's shrill voice carried over the hubbub of setup.

"I'll give you a call when they say they're done with Mom's place. You will come, won't you?"

"Yes, luv. I said I'd be there, and be there I shall." Mary-Margaret gave Chrystal's arm a reassuring squeeze. "Now let me see what the business is in the parking lot."

"It's five dollars to park, Monique. That's just how it is this year. Laura-Jean McQueen said so. Ah," Norman Goodier said, seeing Mary-Margaret approach, "Father Miguel said you'd be moving your car. Thank you. Or would you like to pay the five dollars to park it there?"

"Norman, there are many things here at the church that I would gladly give money to, but parkin' me car in the lot as per the orders of her highness, Laura-Jean McQueen, is not one of them."

"And since when is Laura-Jean McQueen running things here?" Monique demanded. "First, we have Jane Ann murdered, and now we're supposed to pay for parking at our own church bazaar. What's becoming of us all?"

"Well, I can't speak to Jane Ann's death, but—" Norman said.

"Well, I certainly can," chimed Irene Ashford. "It's the boyfriend they're looking at."

"And ye would know this how?" Mary-Margaret asked.

"It's common knowledge, Mary-Margaret. Everyone at the co-op is talking about it. None of us liked him. He just came out of nowhere—swooped in, really, with his bags of half-priced cookies and that little car of his—and then Jane Ann's suddenly not coming to our potlucks or attending the planning meetings or—"

"Sounds like she got a life," Norman said with a chuckle.

"Easy for you to laugh, Norman. Domestic homicide is the number one killer of women in this country."

"That so? I would have thought it would have been heart attacks stemming from obesity, judging by the looks of our congregation."

"Ye may wish to keep yer thoughts to yerself now, Norman," Mary-Margaret suggested in a low tone.

"I heard that the new boyfriend has skipped town. That's what they call it, isn't it? Skipped?" Monique looked at Mary-Margaret.

"I don't think he skipped town, but I do know that they towed his car away. Going to check for blood, I heard. If that doesn't sound guilty, I don't know what does," Irene continued.

"Do they know why he might have done it?" Mary-Margaret asked.

"Jealousy. Violent rage. There never really is a reason in these cases, is there?" Irene said.

"Have they interviewed all of the neighbors?" Mary-Margaret asked.

"I assume so."

"Well, that's somethin'."

"I bet that neighbor next door had some idiotic things to say."

"And ye would say this why?"

"Well, maybe I shouldn't say anything at all, but I'm just thinking about how Jane Ann had told me how she began feeling uncomfortable around him after he moved in and they became chummy. Maybe she knew something about him...."

"So ye have been in touch with Jane Ann since she left the church? And here's me, thinkin' she was livin' happily ever after in her fancy downtown condo all this time."

"There is a life outside of St. Francis', Mary-Margaret," Irene tutted.

"Never said nary a word about her fall from grace when I called her to ask her to help out."

"Living in a co-op is hardly a fall—" Monique began.

"'Tis when ye were living the life o'—"

"Excuse me, ladies, but can you move your gab session somewhere else? I'm trying to run a parking lot here," Norman said. "But before you do, you're both going to have to pony up the five dollars or move your cars."

"As if anyone is going to pay five dollars to park at a church bazaar." Irene laughed.

"Norman, move out of the way! You're going to get run over with a table there," a man hollered good-naturedly from his car.

"That will be five dollars, Eric!" Norman called back.

"For what? To park? I would have thought a guy like you would be rolling in dough after selling your house. Now move your table."

"I'm serious. And it's for the bazaar."

"I'm not paying for parking."

"And I'm not letting you park for free."

"Oh, lads," Mary-Margaret said. "This isn't going to go well, is it?"

"You're in charge, Mary-Margaret. What do you say?" Eric called from his car.

"I say ye park and spend yer fiver on the coffee and biscuits that Joanne is sellin' over there," Mary-Margaret directed.

"But what about my parking job?" Norman asked. "Laura-Jean said—"

"I don't give a pig's foot what Laura-Jean has said or did not say, Norman. As ye can see, her daft plan is causin' ye nothin' but trouble. So everythin' is status quo. Parkin' is free. Coffee, biscuits, and everythin' else is not. And I'll see what I can do about getting' some raffle tickets for ye to sell."

"But what about Laura-Jean?"

"Send her to me if there's any questions. Right. Now, about this neighbor, Irene. Ye were sayin'?

"Well, like I said, I don't actually know, Mary-Margaret. I just know that Jane Ann thought he was odd towards the end…. And, if there's anyone who knows about men, it was Jane Ann."

"Mary-Margaret!" Father Miguel shouted from the church steps. "May I have a word? Inside?"

"Ach, I've got to get the raffle tickets goin'. Just a moment, Father!" Mary-Margaret called back.

"Now." Father Miguel said. He was flanked by Laura-Jean McQueen.

"Oh, me stars. Alright, I'll be right there." She made her way to the church and then, with a smile, added, "Shall I move me car?"

"No need to move your car, Mary-Margaret. Just come inside, please."

* * *

"Please sit down. Both of you," Father Miguel said, pointing at the chairs in front of his desk.

"I've only got this wee moment to sit, Father. Norman needs some raffle tickets to sell."

"No, Norman needs to get people to pay for parking," Laura-Jean said.

"That's not going to happen, luv. I know ye meant well, but as Father Miguel will tell ye, the road to Hell is paved with good intentions. Now if ye'll excuse me, I'll be on me way."

"Sit," Father Miguel repeated sternly.

Mary-Margaret sat.

"Now, ladies, it seems to me that there is a bit of a conflict here."

"Not at all, Father. I'm runnin' me bazaar, as I have done before ye were weein' in the jacks by yerself, and now it's what we in the bazaar business call Show Time. If ye'll excuse me."

"If you will recall, Mary-Margaret, you retired from your position—"

"If ye will recall, Father, ye brought me back. To run the bazaar. Which I have been tryin' to do, despite the mess The New Girl has left ye in, a murder within yer flock, and the meddlin' of Miss Fancy Pants beside me. And, of course, let's not forget me broken foot."

"Your foot is no more broken than—" Laura-Jean began.

"I think we can leave the discussion about your foot out of this, Mary-Margaret, and stick to the point—"

"Which is that there are dozens of people in our back lot right now wantin' to win somethin' in the raffle and Norman has no tickets to sell them."

"Because there is no raffle!" Laura-Jean shrieked.

"Ye see, Father? She's all well and fine until she's not. Poor lamb. I'm sure a cuppa would help, if ye want to get the kettle goin' while I get out and do me job. Now, if ye'll excuse me, if memory serves correct and The New Girl hasn't chucked them, there are a few rolls of unused raffle tickets from the last bazaar in the top right drawer of me desk."

Mary-Margaret did not wait for an answer as she hurried to her former office to look for the tickets.

"Oh, and Father," she called back down the hall, "be sure to use the kettle I've brought in. That other thing might be lovely for coffee, but a real cuppa takes five minutes to steep!"

Chapter Eighteen

"Michael," Mary-Margaret said, panting as she let herself in the back door. "Put us on a kettle."

"Are you okay, Mom?" Michael asked, closing the fridge door.

"Barely. I was almost run off the road."

"Where?"

"Jesus, Mary, and Joseph, lad. On the roadway."

"I got that," Michael said, taking a deep breath, turning the burner on under the kettle. "Which roadway."

"Near the co-op—"

"I thought I said—"

"On me way home from the church, Michael," Mary-Margaret said as she made her way past Michael and through the dining room into the living room, where she dropped heavily into the nearest chair.

"Oh. Did you get a look at the car?" Michael called to her.

"Hardly. I'm lucky to have escaped an early grave," she called back.

Michael poked his head around the wall that divided the kitchen from the rest of the main floor rooms.

"And what is that about, me son? Here's me, tellin' ye about how some maniac was tryin' to run me off the road, and ye are givin' me the stink eye?"

"Do you honestly believe it was intentional?"

"Yes, Michael. I do. There's no other word for it. I was drivin' in me own lane when I see this car in me rearview, racin' up behind me. There's a car in front of me, but, thanks be to God Himself, no traffic goin' the other way. I tap me breaks, just enough to get me red lights flashin', but 'tis no use. I decide to pull into the other lane, and slow right down so's that maniac would have to fly by me. Curious thing, me son: the car slowed well enough when it came up on the car that was in front of me before I pulled out."

"Did you notice the color of the car? The make? Did you get a look at the driver, or get the plate number?"

"Ach, me stars, Michael," Mary-Margaret said with a shiver. "'Twas all I could do to remember to pull back into me own lane and make me way home."

The kettle screamed and Michael tucked himself back into the kitchen to make the tea and get a few cookies onto a plate.

Michael set the tea and cookies on the table beside her.

"Are ye havin' a cuppa as well then, Michael?" Mary-Margaret asked.

"No. I'm off to work in a couple of minutes, but I'm wondering if this has anything to do with your involvement in this murder investigation."

"Are you tryin' to scare me, Michael? And some worry if yer all about tearin' off and leavin' me here alone."

"I'm not trying to scare you. I'm just saying—"

"Grand. And since when does road rage on a Sunday equal a targeted threat on yer mam?"

"I'm not saying that it is. I'm just saying that someone has murdered Jane Ann Hill, and you seem to be taking a particular interest in finding out who, so just maybe—"

"And if ye do think I was targeted, me son," Mary-Margaret said with a chuckle, "I'm sure Jane Ann's killer is not the only one who would like to make short work of me."

"I'm glad you think this is funny, Mom, but if you'd seen your face—"

"A cuppa and a wee biscuit solves everythin'."

"Mom, you're...we're...Detective Gill is investigating a murder, which is serious business. Police business. Business that is not yours."

Just then, Phil came running down the stairs and bounced onto Mary-Margaret's lap.

"Ah, the wee pup," she cooed, giving that spot behind his ear a good scratch

97

before he hopped off her lap and ran towards the back door.

"Why is that dog still here?" Michael asked, looking towards the kitchen.

"Sally-next-door's wee dog? Do ye really need to know right now? I thought ye had to get to yer policin'." She closed her eyes as she rotated her shoulders backwards and forwards. "And besides, the logic be—"

"There is no logic behind this, Mom," Michael interrupted. "That dog peed on my bed while I was in the shower getting ready for work today."

"Ach, that's because he senses that ye don't like him, poor wee thing."

"I don't. And I think it's time for him to go home. It's bad enough—"

"Well, there's yer troubles, then. If ye would like him, then he won't piddle on yer bed. I'm supposin' he needs a walk?"

"I don't have time to take him now."

"I wasn't suggestin' ye did. I'll—"

"Your foot isn't broken, is it, Mom?"

"I'm not a doctor, Michael."

Michael shook his head and looked down at his watch. "I have to go."

"Since ye'll be there anyway, me son, I was wonderin': if I give ye a name or two, can ye check them out on yer computers?"

"Absolutely not."

"Why?"

"Because that's confidential information. For police eyes only. You know that!"

"Well, ye are the police. And I am a part of ye, technically."

"I can't run names, Mom. And you're not getting any more involved in that investigation."

"Apparently, I already am. At least, someone thinks I am, as per yer own observations."

"They're wrong, though, aren't they? And, if they're not, I'm telling you to stop. Now."

"Do ye talk to criminals like that, Michael?"

"Mom."

"I'll turn everythin' I find out over to ye," she said, leaning towards him. "And ye could tell yer Mister Gill that ye figured it out. Might get you a spot in Homicide."

"I don't want a spot in Homicide. And you're not going anywhere near that investigation."

Mary-Margaret's cell phone began to ring. She leaned to one side to pull it out of her pants pocket.

"Hello, luv.... Yes, I'm just this moment havin' a chat with me Michael, but I'll absolutely be there shortly.... Yes, that would be grand.... I don't think he'll come with me, no.... Right. Bye-bye bye bye-bye-bye ."

"And who was that?"

"I've asked ye before, and I see I'll have to ask ye again: Can't a grown woman have a private conversation in this house, Michael?"

"I'm just worried about you, Mom."

"Ye are soundin' like yer sister now. What, might I ask, is there to worry about?"

"I am not sounding like Teaszy. And somebody has just tried to kill you."

"Was a bad driver," Mary-Margaret corrected.

"That's not what you said when you came in—"

"I was clearly confused."

"Regardless, somebody has killed Jane Ann. I'm worried that if you get involved, not only will you mess up the investigation, you might actually get yourself killed."

"I appreciate yer concern, Michael." Mary-Margaret took a sip of her tea. "Well done, lad. Ye must be usin' the Barry's that Max and I brought over from me house. Speakin' of which, where is the wee lamb?"

"At a friend's. Had a sleepover last night."

"But it's almost five now. Shouldn't he be home?"

"His sleepovers seem to last all weekend."

"I'll take Phil out meself for a good walk."

"Phil needs to go back to Sally-next-door."

"Surely we can have that discussion another day, me son." Then, setting her mug on the side table, Mary-Margaret hoisted herself up from her chair. "I'm off now."

"But I thought you were exhausted. And that Phil needed a walk. And you've barely touched your tea."

"And I thought ye were on the verge of bein' late for work."

"You're up to something, aren't you, Mom."

"Hardly. I'm off to for dinner with Francis. I may be late, dependin' on whether Chrystal Hill gives me a ring while I'm at dinner."

"Why would she call you?" Michael said, looking at his watch again as he stood up.

"She's asked me to help get the estate in order." Mary-Margaret walked into the kitchen.

"And if she calls, you're going to go into the apartment, aren't you?" Michael followed her to the kitchen.

"Don't be dim, Michael," his mother said, giving her mug a quick wash. "Of course I would be. Where else would the papers she'll be needin' be?"

"Didn't I just finish saying that you need to stay away from this investigation?"

Ignoring his words, she dried her hands on a tea towel as she looked around the room for her purse. "Ach. There 'tis. Thought I was losing me mind, did I. In the meantime, Michael, maybe I'll call Mandy to see if she can help me out, since ye are not willin'."

And with that, Mary-Margaret was out the back door and sitting behind the wheel of her car.

"Mom, I'm telling you—" Michael called out.

"Ach! Wee Phil!" she said, noticing that she had forgotten about the dog, and saw that he had rushed out with her and was now down the laneway. She rolled down her window. "Michael, before ye leave, make sure ye get Sally-next-door's dog back into the house."

Before Michael could answer, Mary-Margaret had backed Daphne out of the small parking spot and was gone.

Chapter Nineteen

"For someone who's been at a church bazaar all day, ye look ravishing, Mary-Margaret," Frank said, rising from his chair and walking around the table to pull out Mary-Margaret's.

"Ravished is more like it. And ye are full of malarkey. But feel free to carry on," she said with a smile, putting her cheek out for him to kiss before settling herself.

"I've taken the liberty of orderin' ye yer usual," he said, pointing to the half pint of crown float that sat on the table beside his pint of Guinness.

"Ach. Ye are a gift from the heavens, Francis."

"Thought you could use one."

"Sláinte," Mary-Margaret said.

"Sláinte."

The two sat in silence for a moment, savoring their drinks while giving their menus a passing glance.

"Since ye are not after me body, Mary-Margaret," Frank continued with a grin, "I'm going to jump right into me news."

"Do tell."

"Before I start, ye do know, of course, that this is all confidential information. I have a sworn duty not to discuss anythin' that comes across me table with anyone. If ye repeat it and it gets back that I told ye, I will deny everythin'."

"Francis, me son is a police detective. The amount of confidential information that he shares with me over a cuppa in the mornin' would curl yer toes. I think I'm a pretty safe bet, so let's have at it."

"Excuse me, but are you ordering food tonight or just drinks?" a particularly young-looking server asked. "If you need a couple more minutes to look over the menu—"

"Ye are new, aren't ye?" Mary-Margaret said, giving Frank a wink as she passed her menu to the server. "I'll have the shepherd's pie. Tell them at the back that it's for Mary-Margaret and to go light on the salt."

"And I'll have the steak-and-kidney." Frank handed his menu to the girl.

"I would think, with all that ye see, that ye'd steer clear of such things," Mary-Margaret said, half-joking.

"It dusna bother me a bit. Speakin' of which, we were talkin' at the morgue about that autopsy we did on Jane Ann the other day."

"Ye work Saturdays, do ye?"

"Death never sleeps."

"It's an odd line of work ye are in, I'll give ye that." She took a sip of her crown float. "So, what of our girl?"

"Well, as ye can imagine from what I told ye," Frank began, leaning in towards Mary-Margaret, his voice lowering, "'twas not a pretty sight. As an experienced technician, I can handle it, of course, but a lesser man would ha' been brought to the ground."

"I'm sure he would," she said, nodding knowingly. "Cause of death was stabbin', yeah?"

"Not just stabbed. Fourteen times stabbed.

"So ye had said. Seems a bit...excessive."

"Well, I'm not a psychologist, but I've seen me share of such t'ings, and let me assure you, Mary-Margaret, if I were a betting man, and I'm not, I'd lay me money on this bein' a crime of passion."

"Passion? Sounds more like a crime of hate."

"Opposin' side of the same coin, me luv."

"Shepherd's pie?" the young server asked, offering up the warm plate while balancing her tray and its contents in her other hand.

"Here. And steak-and-kidney there," Mary-Margaret directed.

"Ta, luv," Frank said, leaning back while the server placed his dinner in front of him.

Mary-Margaret waited till the server had walked away from the table before continuing. "I suppose ye are right about the coin. So are we thinkin' a boyfriend or somethin' of the sort?"

"I'd say."

"Or could it be a desperate man—or woman—who got carried away?"

"Unlikely just a case of gettin' carried away, luv."

Mary-Margaret took a bite of her dinner.

"And we can say conclusively that the killer was left-handed," Frank added with a knowing nod. He quickly chewed and then swallowed before taking a gulp of Guinness. He then hoisted another forkful of food into his mouth, this time chewing and swallowing before continuing. "Ye see, if the wound is straight on, then the stabber was likely standin' in front o' the person at th' time o' the attack, and given that most o' the world is right-handed," he paused to take another gulp of his beer, "the assumption is that the killer would also be right-handed. If, however, the wound veers t' one side or t'other, ye can conclusively say that the stabber was right- or left-handed, dependin' on the angle of the wound. And with fourteen wounds t' examine, ye get a real sense, if ye will, of how the lad is goin'." With that, he inhaled his final forkful of food.

"Have ye not been feedin' yerself, me lad? I've not seen anyone eat that fast since Max's last growth spurt," Mary-Margaret commented, looking across the table.

"Apologies, me luv," Frank said, a slight redness coming to his cheeks. "I get a wee bit excited when I'm talkin' about me work, and everythin' just speeds up."

"I admire a man who feels passionately about his work," Mary-Margaret said, nodding in approval.

"Do ye, now?" Frank asked, looking across the table at Mary-Margaret. "There's another passion in me life, don'tcha know?"

"I'm sure ye are a man of many passions, Francis," Mary-Margaret smiled, "but, gettin' back to the business at hand, from what I'm gatherin, I can go about lookin' for a left-handed killer?"

"Definitely left-handed," Frank answered with a slow exhale. "And money on 't, 'tis a lad yer after."

"Why?"

"Some of those wounds went almost through her body. No woman would have t' strength t' do that sort o' damage."

"Not even a jealous woman?"

"Unlikely."

"Ye don't know the wrath of a woman, do ye, Francis?" Mary-Margaret said with a wink, polishing off her dinner.

"I canna speak to that, Mary-Margaret, but I will say that a woman doesn't have the upper body strength of a man."

"Is that so?" Mary-Margaret said, glancing over at Maeve O'Leary, the co-owner of the pub, who was balancing a tray with ten pints of beer on it with one hand while opening the gate from behind the bar with another.

"Well, let's just say it's nay the usual."

"And do we know where the body was found?"

"That I can answer conclusively," Frank said. "Outside. Likely dumped. T' were leaves and the like in her hair, but nothin' 'bout the body suggestin' she was alive while in t' ravine."

"Ravine?"

"Confidential!" Frank said, his cheeks reddening.

"You know me," Mary-Margaret said, pulling her thumb and index finger along her closed lips. "So was she dead before she got to the ravine, or died once she got there?"

"Dead or close t' it by t' time she got there."

"And so she did struggle, then?"

"Likely quite t' fight, did yer girl put up. But not while she was at t' ravine."

"And ye know this how?"

"We found quite a bit o' skin under her nails and nothin' t' do with leaves or mud or anythin' o' that sort, which would o' been there if she'd been fightin' fer her life at t' ravine." Frank was quiet for a moment before adding: "Nasty stuff, Mary-Margaret. Let's leave tha' bit well enough alone, shall we?"

"Of course," Mary-Margaret said, surprised that an experienced autopsy technician would find anything off-putting.

"Whoever did it t' her was likely not as tall as she."

"And ye would know how tall he is from the stab wounds as well?"

"Exactly. And he's likely an A Positive blood type."

"Well, that's hardly helpful, is it?"

"Rules out the A negs, all o' the B's, and the O's. That's summat," he said with a sniff.

"I suppose. And how would ye be knowing the blood type of our killer?"

"Will you be having dessert this evening, or can I get you another drink?" the server asked as she came up behind Mary-Margaret.

"Oh, my good glory. I didn't see ye behind me, luv!" Mary-Margret said with a start. "I believe we are fine. Francis?"

"That will be it for me, luv. Just the bill?"

"You bet," the girl said, hurrying away as quietly as she had approached.

"I don't know if it's just me nerves or the girl moves like a wee fairy. She almost scared the bejeebers out of me!"

"Murder isna for everyone, Mary-Margaret. Perhaps ye'd be best t' be leavin' it—"

"Francis, if one more person suggests I leave it, I'll scream right here and now! I wasn't goin' to take this on—the good Lord knows I've got enough on me plate, what with me Michael and his troubles, and Sally-next-door's dog, and the mess Father Miguel and The New Girl are makin' of the church, not to mention that daft Laura-Jean McQueen—"

"So ye are takin' it on then?"

"Obviously. Now tell me about this blood type?"

"I may kick meself later, but I'll help ye as I am able. T'ing about blood: transfers from one t' another. Called blood transference. Yer girl was an O blood type. There were traces of A Positive under her nails."

"So ye would likely have enough to find out the DNA of the killer if ye found somethin' under her nails?"

"Likely, but that will take time. All I'm sayin' now is that our killer is male, likely her height, with A pos blood, and would have some scratches on his body. Likely his face or arms."

"A regular Sherlock Holmes ye are," Mary-Margaret said admiringly.

"Ye could say as much, yes. Ye know, I have testified at more than a few homicide trials in me day."

"Have ye, then? Well, I'm thinkin' ye would know me Mandy."

"And who might she be when she's at work, now?"

"Detective Amanda Black. She's in the homicide squad."

"Oh, Detective Black. Yes. I know her. We call her the pit bull in stilettos at the morgue."

"Is that a good thing or a bad thing?"

"'Tis very good. I wouldna wan' her handlin' me case if I were a murderer."

"I'll let her know then, shall I?"

"I'd rather ye not. I've seen more than a few homicide detectives get too big fer their britches over t' years. And then they're of no use to anyone, nay even the dead."

"Was it that awful, Frank?"

"Was what?"

"The way she—Jane Ann—looked?"

"Even though I've seen 't all on me table over me time at the morgue , I'd have to say yeah."

In that moment he looked like a little boy to Mary-Margaret.

"Ye are a prince of a man, Francis."

"If that were the case, then why are we nay snugglin' somewhere rather than havin' a pint an' some crisps after all these years?"

"Ach, Francis. It's not you, luv. It's—"

"Ye?"

"No. It's not me, either. Wish it was. It's Jimmy, God rest his soul."

"God rest his soul."

"He was the love of me life." Mary-Margaret wiped at her eye.

"And there's been no one since him?"

"Not that mattered." She looked around her to make sure no one saw her moment of weakness.

"So why not me?"

She laughed merrily. "Because, ye silly bastard, ye matter."

"Should I take that as a compliment?"

106

"Yes, Francis, a compliment of the highest order. Now it's gettin' on, and I've got a big day tomorrow, it bein' Sunday and all."

"Of course," he said. "Leave the bill-payin' to me. My treat. Whether ye know it or not, ye have given me the highest praise a man could ever receive."

"And ye don't have to pay for it. We'll split the bill, as we always have. Here's our girl now." She reached up for the bill. "Ta, luv."

Chapter Twenty

"May Almighty God bless you—the Father, the Son, and the Holy Spirit. Go in peace, giving glory to God by your life."

"Ach, I hope Laura-Jean has the coffee and tea ready. There'll be hell to pay if not, judgin' by the size of the congregation today," Mary-Margaret muttered to herself as she made her way to the auditorium for what was known at St. Francis's as The Afterwards.

"Lovely sermon, Father," she said, shaking Father Miguel's hand as she left the narthex.

"May God bless you, Mary-Margaret," Father Miguel replied. "And thank you for your help these past two weeks. You know Ashleigh will be back tomorrow morning, so perhaps you could take whatever you've left in her office home with you when you leave today?"

"Of course, Father. Shall I leave me old kettle out for her, or shall I assume that ye don't provide tea for yer parishioners anymore?"

"Please don't forget your crutches." Father Miguel smiled as he turned to the next person in line. "May God bless you, Monique."

As Mary-Margaret went into the full auditorium, she saw Laura-Jean come bustling out of the adjoining kitchen carrying a huge urn of coffee. The cookies were already out and were surrounded by several parishioners.

"Hot coffee coming through!" Laura-Jean called out as she set the urn on one of the tables near the cookies.

"To think someone from our church would get murdered," Mary Margaret heard one of the elderly parishioners say as she helped herself to some cookies.

"She wasn't actually from this church, was she?" another asked and then looked at Laura-Jean. "No tea today, then?"

"The tea is coming, everyone," Laura-Jean announced over the grumbling of the growing crowd gathering in front of her.

"Used to be a time when the tea was ready before we came in. I guess I'll have to have a decaf coffee instead," a well-dressed man commented as he took a Styrofoam cup filled to the brim with coffee from the table in front of him. "At least, I hope this is decaf. Otherwise, I'll be up all night."

"I'll have to admit, this is a bit of a disappointment," sniffed the second woman. "Is this your first time doing The Afterwards, Laura-Jean? I mean, since your hus...."

The words hung in the air. Everyone knew what she meant.

"Tea is usually already out," the woman continued, "with the cups right there beside the coffee. Just needs to be poured. But, I suppose, when someone in your midst has been murdered, we're allowed to falter. I didn't catch the name."

"Are we talkin' about Jane Ann Hill, then?" Mary-Margaret asked as she approached the refreshment table. "If so, yes, she was a part of our church. For much longer than ye were, I might add. Quite involved until she moved downtown, in fact. And yes, I'd have to agree. This isn't our most efficient Afterwards, is it?"

Laura-Jean pursed her lips and glared at Mary-Margaret.

"It was Jane Ann Hill? Wow. What happened, or do they know?" Norman Goodier asked as he approached the refreshment table.

"Stabbed," Mary-Margaret said, then recalling her promise to Frank just the night before, added, "or somethin' like that."

"Do you know this for a fact, or are you just gossiping?" Laura-Jean asked from behind the table, handing out cups of tea and coffee over the trays of digestive biscuits.

"I am not gossiping," Mary-Margaret said frostily as she took her tea.

"So, how do you know? I haven't seen anything in the papers about it. Or do you have an inside?" Norman asked, and then, with a smile, added: "Your boy's the police detective, isn't he?"

"Indeed, but he wouldn't be tellin' me such things, ye can rest assured, luv."

"So you don't really know," Laura-Jean McQueen said with a sneer. "Cookie?"

"I suppose I don't. And I will help meself to a biscuit, thank ye."

"I just think it's tragic that Jane Ann was murdered," Laura-Jean said, "and then even worse that people are gossiping about it. People like you."

"I'll have ye know, Laura-Jean, that I have been asked by Jane Ann's daughter, no less, to help solve the murder—"

"Because the police can't? Do tell!" a voice called out.

"Because she'll have nothing to do now once Ashleigh gets back, so she's going to meddle in something she knows nothing of," Laura-Jean blurted.

"That's very unchristian of you, Laura-Jean," Irene Ashford said, having overheard the entire conversation.

"Indeed. Which just proves, as everyone standin' here knows, that God reveals all to those who are willing to see," Mary-Margaret said, walking away from the table and her nemesis with her cup of lukewarm tea and a stale biscuit.

"Don't pay any attention to Laura-Jean, Mary-Margaret," Monique Prud-homme said. "We all know she's gone a bit off. Ever since Russ left her."

"In light of the earlier comments about bein' unchristian, I am holdin' me tongue, but I can't say that I blame the man."

"We don't know what happened there, Mary-Margaret. But she's struggling enough without us adding to her burdens."

"Ye are right, of course."

"So are you involved at all with the Exemplary Attendance Awards next week?" Moniqu asked. "Father Miguel didn't make any mention of it, and I was just wondering if we were still going to do it? I don't think Ashleigh will have enough time to get everything in order if she's only back from her honeymoon tomorrow."

"Ach. There's another thing, but I'll hold me tongue. Again. And no, I'm out the door like yesterday's rubbish now that The New Girl is back. Hopefully, she can organize the presentations. It means so much to the young people when they get their crucifixes."

"It is a lovely gesture, although it's not really for exemplary attendance, is it? Doesn't everyone in the confirmation class get one?"

"Indeed, but it's only after completin' the course. All of me children received theirs, except for me Peter, as ye know."

The conversation paused awkwardly. While it wasn't exactly common knowledge that Mary-Margaret's third child had gone off the rails, it wasn't a family secret, either.

"So you are going to find the killer, are you?" Irene returned to the original topic of discussion.

"We shall see, shan't we?"

"Do the police really have nothing to go on?"

"I don't know where they're at, but as me Michael would say, it's early days."

"Early days, my ear," a man chimed in. "We've got a killer on the loose, and they haven't done anything."

"I wouldn't say that, Wayne," Mary-Margaret began.

"You're just saying that because your son is a cop. If it was your mother, you'd feel differently."

She recalled that Wayne had been in Michael's Sunday school class as a boy and, if memory serves, had had more than a few run-ins with the police himself.

"And that's why she's gotten involved," Monique said.

"Well, all I can say is that this is the second murder they've had at that co-op within a few months, maybe a year," he continued.

"A second murder?" Mary-Margaret said, furrowing her brow. "No one's mentioned anythin' about that."

"Pffff. Why would they? Didn't solve that one either. And now there's two old chicks dead. Nobody gives a crap about them. They probably assigned a C-grade cop to 'look into it'. They'll never solve it."

"And ye know this how?" Mary-Margaret challenged.

"Simple. They're cops. Too busy drinking coffee and eating donuts and doing social media bytes to care about people like you."

"Like me?" Mary-Margaret said, pulling herself up even straight while cocking her head to one side.

"Yeah. Old broads with no money and no political pull."

Chapter Twenty-One

A s long as there had been Sundays, there had been dinners at Mary-Margaret's table. Attendance was mandatory, barring death, and even that, as was evidenced by the empty place left at the head of the table for Jimmy O'Shea, was debatable. Except for the anticipated absences due to distance, as in the case of Katie and her partner, Ahmed, the entire O'Shea clan was expected to be in attendance. When Mike was working evening shift, it was not uncommon for him to bring his partner—or the entire team—to dinner as well. And when Petey, her third child, had stopped coming home, Mary-Margaret could not find it in her heart to leave his place empty, so it was set every Sunday, to be known as *The Place For The Unexpected Guest.*

"Michael, pass yer sister some cabbage," Mary-Margaret said. "And while yer at it, be sure to take some for yerself. Is it me cooking, or is everybody off this evening?"

"Gran, I know it's a cultural thing and everything, but do we always have to have corned beef and cabbage on Sundays?" Paulie asked.

If a fork had dropped on the floor in the house next door, everyone at Mary-Margaret's table would have heard it.

"And just what do ye meant by that, lad?" Mary-Margaret asked after a long silence.

"Oh god," Allan sighed. "Here we go."

"Shhh!" Teaszy said, nudging her husband's leg under the table with her knee while giving their son *the look.*

"It's just that, well, nobody really likes corned beef and cabbage," Paulie continued. At twenty-four, he was surprised to hear his voice crack.

"I like it," Max said, smiling at his grandmother, who nodded approvingly at him.

"That's because you're the youngest. Give it another few years," Paulie replied.

"Paulie, are you still seeing that forensics guy? Jorge, was it?" Mike asked.

"Ugh! Do not ever bring up his name, Uncle Mike. I can't believe I ever even kissed him, let alone...you know...," Paulie said, scrunched up his nose, as if a horrid smell had just wafted across the room.

"Really, son?" Allan winced. "Did you have to go there?"

"I believe I've got something for ye in the kitchen," Mary-Margaret said, jumping out of her seat and rushing into the next room.

"Why did you have to say that, Paulie?" Teaszy asked, once she thought that her mother was out of earshot.

"Because it's true. Jorge is—"

"No, about the corned beef," Teaszy clarified.

"Because it's also true. Come on, Mom. How many years have we been having dinner together and how many years has Dad been saying he'd rather eat vomit than this crap?"

"Really?" Teaszy looked over at Allan.

"Well, that's a bit of an exaggeration, I'd say, wouldn't you, Paulie?"

"Maybe a bit, Dad, but—"

"I would strongly suggest you go into the kitchen and apologize to your grandmother," Teaszy interrupted.

"No need to apologize to anyone," Mary-Margaret said, coming back into the dining room carrying a bowl with a slice of iceberg lettuce, a cut-up tomato, and a couple of chunks of a carrot in it. "I knew it all started with ye, Allan, but if ye've poisoned me own grandson against it, I've got a salad here for ye. I'll be gladly eatin' all of the corned beef meself for the week to come, thank ye very much."

Mary-Margaret plunked herself down once again at the head of the table.

"And as for ye, Paulie, if ye have somethin' to say about the menu, I'd appreciate ye tellin' me more than a moment before we eat. Now, Michael, pass me some good Irish food."

Mike passed the plate of corned beef down the table to his mother.

"Can I have some, too, Gran?" Max asked.

"Of course, ye can, me lamb. Have as much as ye want. Apparently, yer aunt and uncle and their child are too good for it."

"Mom," Teaszy moaned.

"And while we're at it, have ye been laid off yet, Allan?"

"I'm not getting laid off, Mary-Margaret."

"So ye think. Ye do know, of course, that me house is sitting empty while I'm here with our Michael. Ye might as well consider sellin' or rentin' yer place and movin' into mine to save yerselves some money."

Mike began to choke on his food, almost spitting it up into his hand before he was able to regain his composure.

"How long were you intending on staying?" Mike asked.

"We don't need to save any money at the moment," Allan said, helping himself to a large portion of salad.

"Suit yerselves, then. And I'll be here until I'm not, Michael. Now, about our murder...."

"What murder?" Mike asked.

"Jane Ann's, of course. Are ye sure ye are good to be goin' back to work so soon after that cloberin', son? Ye don't seem to be followin' along with the convo very well these days."

"I'm sure I'm fine, Mom. And it's not our murder."

"Well, it is now. For all yer lads are doin' about it. Here, Max, help yerself to some of the cabbage. Best I've likely ever made. And ye, Paulie? Are ye not eating the salad now? Too...American...for ye?"

"I'm just not that hungry," Paulie said. "And no salad dressing."

"Great. Practically starts a civil war at the table, and he's not hungry," Allan mumbled into the raw vegetables on his plate.

"I heard that, Allan!" Teaszy said, administering another sharp knock of her knee against his under the table.

"Max, go into yer fridge and pull out the Ranch style dressin' yer da has on the door. I don't know what it tastes like, lads, or if it's expired, but I'm sure it will suit ye fine." Mary-Margaret said.

"Sit," Mike said as Max stood up and then sat down quickly on his chair. "Don't get involved."

"As ye please," Mary-Margaret said, looking directly at Mike. "Now, Jane Ann's murder, Michael. What do we know of it?"

"Nothing, Mom. We don't know anything."

"Clearly. Which is why I'm taking it over."

For the second time this particular evening, the sound of a fork dropping anywhere in the neighbourhood could have been heard by everyone at the table.

"Pardon?" Mike finally said, clearing his throat.

"Ye heard me, lad. I'm takin' over the investigation. Not professionally, of course, but on me own time. Seems yer lot are too busy doin' whatever it is ye do. I wish our Mandy was in charge. She'd have the thing sewn up and sent to the cleaners by now. As it stands, the murderer is likely laughin' in his pint right now, watchin' the bumbleheads that are runnin' this show."

"And just how do you intend to 'take over' this investigation, Mom?"

"I've got me sources. And me people. Kind of like yer Nancy Drew back in the day, really."

"More like Miss Marple without her marbles," Allan chuckled before wincing as his wife gave him a very swift knock to his already tender knee.

"Not at all like Nancy Drew back in any day, Mom. This is real life. A woman is dead and someone murdered her. Someone dangerous."

"Ooooh," Mary-Margaret said mockingly. "The Big City Detective is warnin' the countryfolk about the bad people that wander amongst us."

"I'm not kidding, Mom. This is dangerous stuff. Trust me."

"Ach, lad, it's not about trust. It's about findin' out who killed Jane Ann. Even before I decided to take the case on—"

"You did not take the case on."

"Even before I decided to take the case on, I likely knew more than yer lads. And now, with Chrystal's help—"

"Mom, I've told you before, Detective Gill has told you, and now he's telling me to tell you: Stay out of it. Otherwise, you're obstructing justice."

"As if there will be any justice at the rate your Detective Billy Gilly and his lads are goin'."

"Nevertheless, leave it."

"And do ye know, Clever Clogs, that there was another woman murdered in that same co-op?"

"It's not my case, or yours, so just leave it alone."

"I was the first one to see the murder scene, ye know." Mary-Margaret said with a nod, beaming at her family.

"Eww. Was it horrible, Gran? Like on TV?" Paulie asked, absently poking at the food on his plate.

"I'll not be discussing what I saw at the dinner table, luv, but rest assured, it was unpleasant."

"Mom, this is not a game."

"And who's sayin' it is, me son?"

"Or something to be discussed over dinner," Allan pointed out.

"Can a woman not choose what she wishes to discuss at her own family dinner table without a man shuttin' her down? Surely, we've come past those days, have we not, or is this how 'tis at yer house, Teaszy?"

"I don't think that's what Allan is saying," Teaszy began.

'Well, what is he sayin'? Yer all about talking up a storm until yer wife knocks ye under the table, but ye need yer wife to speak for ye when ye know ye've gone too far."

"I didn't think—" Allan sputtered.

"Clearly not. Regardless, if it's all the same to ye, I think I'll just be retirin' for the evenin'. Max, luv, could you make sure that wee Phil goes out for a piddle before bed, then? Right, I'm off. Teaszy, can ye clean up for me? And Michael, me foot is achin' as if the young lad from The Maquires has been pounding on it all night. Help me upstairs, will ye?"

"I've got to get back to wo—"

"Never mind, then. I'll just make me way and hope I don't trip and fall to me death. Max, can ye find me crutches, lad?"

"Mom," Mike sighed, defeated. "I'll help you. And they have a suspect in mind on the case, so can you just leave it?"

"I can't speak of it now. Me ankle—"

"Isn't it your foot, Mom?" Teaszy asked.

"Ach, if yer da, God rest his soul, was here, he'd have something to say to the lot of ye."

"And he'd be telling you to keep your nose out of this, Mom," Mike said, getting up from the table.

"Yer da, God rest his soul, would never say such a thing. And if he did, I'd be tellin' him that we'll not be speakin' of it, or anythin' else, again tonight. So, Michael, since ye are in such a rush to get back to your policin', don't worry about helpin' yer old mam up the steep stairs to the tiny room she has been shoved into whilst givin' up her own independence to care for her eldest child. No, lads, I shall hope the wee people will smile upon me as I stumble me way towards me bed."

Chapter Twenty-Two

I t was with more than the slightest bit of satisfaction that Mary-Margaret rapped on the open door of Father Miguel's office shortly after 11 the following morning.

"Yes. Well. You're here," he said with a sigh.

Mary-Margaret stood, looking down at the young priest, waiting. When nothing happened, she turned on her heel and walked up the hallway to her former office.

"You're welcome," she muttered,

It would seem that The New Girl had not returned this morning for reasons that were unknown to Mary-Margaret.

Of all the days....

From her own experiences, Mary-Margaret knew that missing a day or two here or there was not an issue at St. Francis of Assisi, but this, being the day right after the bazaar, was a day not to be missed. All the cash from the bazaar would have been shoved into a large brown envelope and left in the church secretary's office in a box under the desk. The items that were not sold would have been hastily thrown back into the parlor, and there would no doubt be food items that never made it out to the various tables left sitting to either rot in the fridge or be given to children in the daycare downstairs.

Not the day, New Girl. Not the day.

Thankful that she had not taken her kettle home with her yesterday, Mary-Margaret pulled a bag of Barry's tea that she always had in her purse for such impromptu occasions. And, while she waited for the kettle to boil,

119

she couldn't help feeling just the slightest bit of satisfaction knowing that, despite her youth and, Mary-Margaret was sure, her outgoing personality, The New Girl was no match for the likes of her.

"Oh," Laura-Jean said, her shoes squeaking on the polished tile floor as she came to an abrupt stop just inside the office.

"Oh yerself," Mary-Margaret said with a start.

"I—I just thought, you know, that—"

"That ye'd take over me job even still?" Mary-Margaret said, looking squarely at Laura-Jean McQueen.

"No. Not in the least," Laura-Jean replied, her cheeks flushing. "I just thought that Ashleigh would be—"

"Would be what? Here? Rememberin' that she's got work to do? That the honeymoon doesn't last forever? That, even after the smashing success that she would have to have known the bazaar would be, there was work to be done?"

Mary-Margaret's back was straight, her shoulders back, as she stood almost toe-to-toe with Laura-Jean.

"No. I mean, yes. I mean…I'm so sorry, Mary-Margaret."

"'Tis all forgiven. Ye aren't in yer right mind, as we all know. And, of course, ye'd want to take over the bazaar. Done properly, it looks so simple. 'Tis part of the magic of it all, I suppose."

"No, I—"

The kettle began to whistle.

"But, since ye are here, there's work to be done. Ye can start by sortin' what's left of the clothin' into two lots: one for the binman, one for charity. Keep yer eye on the clock and, when it gets closer to lunch—ach, look at the time. Never mind the sortin' at this moment. Get the food out of the fridge and take it downstairs. Let them eat what they want, then go down at 1:30, bring the trays back up, and toss what's left. Unless ye what to pick over what the little hands have already mauled."

Laura-Jean nodded several times as the whistle of the kettle intensified.

"And then, when ye're done that, sort the clothes in the parlor. I'll be here if ye need me, lookin' after the more advanced workin's of the bazaar."

120

"I just want to say again how sorry I am that—"

"Water under the bridge, luv. Now, get yer skates on, and away ye go!"

With that, Laura-Jean practically ran out of the office.

Odd wee soul, that one.

* * *

After counting all the money, preparing the bank deposit slip, putting it back in the envelope, and depositing it in the safe for someone from the Treasury Committee to pick up and take to the bank at some later date, Mary-Margaret looked down at her watch.

Seeing that Laura-Jean would likely just be picking up the trays from downstairs and would then be otherwise occupied for some time, Mary-Margaret reached into her purse and pulled out the library card from the wallet left by the young man who had tried to break into her car the other night.

"West End Branch, Caitlin at the library speaking," a small, cheery voice said on the other end of the phone line.

"Yes, well, hello," Mary-Margaret replied, stretching the cord from the desk phone as far as it would go as she looked out into the empty hallway before turning the lock on the office door. "I was wonderin' if ye could provide me with a bit of information."

"Certainly, ma'am. What type of book are you interested in?"

"'Tis not a book that I'm lookin' for. 'Tis...me grandson."

"I'm sorry?"

"Yes, uh, it seems that I've lost his phone number, but I know he has a library card, and I was hopin' that, if I give ye his name, ye can reach into yer files and get his number for me."

"Oh, I'm sorry, ma'am, but we aren't allow—"

"I know, luv, but it's...urgent. Ye see, I'm his gran. And there's been a bit of a family...disaster."

No response.

"I need to contact wee Bobbo," Mary-Margaret said, her voice quivering.

121

"He's got to know about…the horror that has befallen—"

"Just a minute. I'll get my supervisor," the young girl said, the pitch of her voice rising even higher than it had previously been.

"No time for that, luv," Mary-Margaret quickly whispered. "I've only just got a few moments of time left. Can ye just blurt it out quickly and—"

"I'm not even sure I know how to get phone numbers out of the system," she replied.

"It canna be that hard, luv, and ye sound like a clever lass. I'll wait while ye figure it out."

There was a pause.

"But I canna wait too long on account of me," Mary-Margaret began tapping the receiver of the phone with the palm of her hand. "Not much life left in the old girl."

"One moment."

"What's yer name again, luv?"

"Caitlin."

"Ye are a lifesaver, Cait—" Mary-Margaret tapped the receiver another few times. "Not much time left."

"Hang on," the young girl said. Mary-Margaret could hear frantic tapping on a keyboard.

"Not. Much," whap whap whap whap, "left."

"What's his name?" Caitlin called out, sounding more like a triage nurse on the front lines than a part-time librarian on a Monday afternoon.

"Bobbo. Robert. Robert Jackson."

"Hmmm. There are a few Robert Jacksons here. What's his address?"

"I dunna know, luv. He's fallen on hard times. It wouldn't surprise me if he was homeless. And, for such a young lad. Tsk tsk tsk. Likely just around yer own age. A right pain in his mam's heart, has this caused her. Before the disaster of which I'm callin' struck, of course."

"Of course. I understand. I do have a number for a Robert Jackson with a date of birth—"

"No. Time," Mary-Margaret choked, grabbing a pen and paper from her former desk.

Caitlin yelled the phone number to Mary-Margaret.

* * *

"Yeah?" an annoyed young man answered.

"Bobbo?"

"Huh?"

"I mean Robert?"

"Yeah."

"Robert Anderson?"

"Who's askin'?"

"Mary-Margaret…yer social worker."

"I don't have a social worker."

"Before ye hang up," Mary-Margaret quickly said, realizing that this was her only chance to speak to the young man, "ye, in fact, do. I'm…court appointed."

"Say what?"

"Ye know as well as I that ye have been in and out of the courts over the last wee while. And the judge is getting' tired of seein' yer mug," Mary-Margaret reclined into her chair and settled into it and her new personae, hopeful that her suspicions about the young man would be true. "So he's appointed me to keep an eye on ye."

"So what?"

"So ye need to come and speak to me to get some…things…settled."

Mary-Margaret could hear the young man breathing heavily on the other end of the line.

"I'll tell ye what, lad. Meet me in the office at St. Francis of Assisi's. Ye know where it is, don't ye? Bein' a west-end lad and all?"

"Yeah. Yeah. I know where that is. When?"

"Meet me there," Mary-Margaret looked at her watch, "in thirty minutes."

"Thirty minutes?" Robert balked.

"And yer tellin' me that ye've got an appointment for anything else today, lad?"

"No. No. I'll be there. Thanks."

"Grand," she said and slammed down the phone.

Mary-Margaret sat at the desk for a moment. And then she stood up. And then she sat down again.

Ye may have gone too far this time, she thought to herself. What if he's a maniac?

Mary-Margaret stood up again.

Ach, there's nothin' for it but to call Arthur.

* * *

"Arthur, I need you to come right now," whispered Mary-Margaret.

"MM?"

"Well, who else would it be?" she practically hollered.

"Where are you?"

"I'm in me office—me old office—at the church. I've got a maniac comin' in to see me in thirty minutes."

"Why?"

"Is this the Inquisition? Just get yerself here, lad!"

"I'm on my way," he replied.

Mary-Margaret hung up the phone and walked over to the kettle. It was out of water. Sensing it was too risky to try to make a break for the kitchen with Laura-Jean McQueen wandering about, she gave up the notion of a soothing cuppa, locked the office door, and sat down, losing her eyes to try to settle her nerves.

* * *

"Sister Augustine, at your service."

"Ach!" Mary-Margaret screamed, waking up from her nap to see a huge figure covered from head to toe by a black cloak.

"MM. It's me. Arthur," he said, dropping to his knees beside her.

"I thought ye was the grim reaper. How did ye get in?"

"Oh, I just picked the lock with a paperclip. Super easy. I didn't even have to break out my—"

"And what in the name of—"

"Isn't it fab? I just happened to have this old nun's habit lying around and never thought I'd ever get the chance to wear it, so when you called...," he concluded, standing up to his full six foot four inches with both arms held out to his side and then giving himself a spin. "Julie Andrews, eat your heart out."

"Don't tell me ye are goin' to sing, lad," Mary-Margaret said, trying to regain her composure.

"Oh," Arthur said with a prolonged sigh, "Sadly, that is one of the many gifts that I do not possess."

"Just as well. Now, how are ye goin' to help me with this sadist I've got comin' to see me?"

"About that," Arthur said, sashaying over to close the office door. "Who is this creep, and why is he coming here?"

"Ach, the logic behind it is too complicated for me mind to unravel to ye in this moment," she said, instinctively walking over to where the kettle should have been and then, recalling that it was no longer there, remained by the window that looked into the unkempt courtyard. I hate to go all Michael on you, MM, but I think I need to know something about what's going on here."

"He's the lad who tried to break into me car the other night at O'Leary's."

"Someone tried to break into Daphne?"

"Indeed. But I chased him off. Luckily, he left his calling card, and here we are."

"Why aren't we letting the police handle this?"

"Ye are goin' all...what was it ye said...Michael...on me, aren't ye?"

There was a sharp knock on the door.

"It's him," Mary-Margaret whispered.

"Come in," Arthur called in an unusually high falsetto while making his way to the door.

"Mary-Ma—" Laura-Jean began as she walked into the office, and then stopped, her jaw dropping.

"And what were ye expectin'?" Mary-Margaret said, regaining her composure. "'Tis a catholic church ye are in, after all."

"No, I-I-I…"

"Now, if ye'll excuse us, me and Sister Augustine have some business to attend to," Mary-Margaret said, stepping between Arthur and Laura-Jean.

"Of course," Laura-Jean said, not moving except to look around Mary-Margaret at the figure in the middle of the room.

"And ye shall be in the parlor doin' the sortin' for the duration?" Mary-Margaret said, taking Laura-Jean by the shoulders and moving her back towards the open door.

"Yes. Yes, of course, I will be. So nice to meet you, Sister…?"

"Augustine. Sister Augustine," Arthur said, holding his head high to display the full force of his habit. "And a blessing upon you."

"And upon you," Laura-Jean stammered as she stepped away from Mary-Margaret and backed out of the room, genuflecting and nodding as she went.

"I was born for this," Arthur said, closing the door behind her. "You know, MM, I may have just found my true calling."

Chapter Twenty-Three

Mary-Margaret plunked herself down on her chair but, before she could respond, there was another knock on the door. This one was harder and not so sharp.

"Oh, for the love of God," Mary-Margaret mumbled, "come in."

"Oh," a scrawny young man mumbled. "Wasn't expecting..."

Mary-Margaret gasped.

"Few people are. Sister Augustine," Arthur said, moving forward as he thrust out his hand.

"Uh, sure. Uh. Rob Anderson."

"Very good, Robert. You don't mind if I call you Robert, do you? No, you don't. Now, I understand you've been breaking into cars?" Arthur said, standing uncomfortably close to the young man.

"Uh, no. Well, yeah. Um, you don't sound like the lady I spoke to on the phone."

"Because I'm not. I would invite you to sit down, but there's nowhere to sit. So, my...church lady friend, here, tells me that you've..."

"I'm supposed to see a social worker," Robert offered.

"Ach, lad," Mary-Margaret said, getting up from her desk chair , holding her hand out for him to shake. "That would be me, Mary-Margaret. Ye will have to forgive Sister Augustine. Her fitted coif comes back a bit too tight from the laundry now and again. Now, have a seat. Here."

With no other viable option, the young man sat down in the chair previously occupied by Mary-Margaret and stared up at her and further up at whom he believed to be the largest nun he'd ever seen.

"Well, ye are probably wonderin' why ye are here," she began, calling upon the dialogue from every detective novel she had ever read. "We, me colleague and I, want to talk to ye about yer goin's on over the past wee while."

"I dunno," he shrugged. "I been around."

"That's your problem, Robert. You've been around a bit too much," Arthur said, his teeth clenched as he leaned in towards the now-quivering man's face.

"Sister Augustine...?" Mary-Margaret said. "Perhaps I'll do the talkin', so?"

"You wouldn't last a day in the convent," Arthur hissed as he moved toward the window ledge, away from Robert and Mary-Margaret.

"What me...what Sister Augustine is tryin' to say, luv, is that we've been seein' an awful lot of ye around these days, and everyone's a bit on edge, what with the unsolved murder—"

"What does that have to do with me?"

"Well, I did see ye on the bus the other day with a sack of belongin's I'm assumin' weren't yours?"

"I don't know what you're talking about."

"And then I saw ye again, on that very same bus route the next mornin', without that sack of belongin's with another lad."

"So?"

"And the two of ye looked quite a bit worse for wear, if ye know what I mean."

"No. I don't."

"Don't make me hurt you," Arthur mouthed from across the room.

The young man shook his head and then looked back at Mary-Margaret.

"What I'm tryin' to say, luv, is that we all know ye stole some things, sold those same things, and then used the proceeds to buy yerselves a wee bit of whisky."

"Or worse," Arthur hissed.

"No," the young man said with a huff, shaking his head.

"Luv, we're no longer talkin' about revokin' yer day pass."

"What day pass? I'm not on a day pass."

"Listen to what the lady's trying to say," Arthur spat.

"I don't know anything about a day pass."

"And I saw ye the other day at the murder scene."

"I swear to god," Rob said, looking frantically back and forth to Mary-Margaret and Arthur. "I had nothing to do with that."

"So ye know about it?"

"Listen, lady—"

"Mary. Margaret," Arthur said between clenched teeth. "Her name is Mary-Margaret, and you will respect her."

"Mary-Margaret. I don't know anything about that. I mean, yeah. I'm a B&E guy. That stuff I had on the bus was from an apartment I broke into. Yeah. But I never killed anyone."

"So what were ye doin' at the co-op?"

Rob sat silently, first staring up at the ceiling, then down at his dirty fingernails.

"Answer her!" Arthur yelled, lunging from his perch on the ledge towards Rob.

"Don't hurt me," the small man said, bringing his arms up to his head as he curled up on the chair.

"Then answer her," Arthur repeated.

"I—I—I was going to break in. I mean, I was going to, but the door was unlocked so I just walked in. And yeah. I was inside, but the place was already trashed when I opened the door. I shoulda just closed it and left then, but I was kinda out of my head, you know, so I thought I'd just take a look inside, maybe see if there was anything worth taking—"

"And you killed her," Arthur said.

"No! No! I didn't kill anyone. I mean, no one was there. I looked inside the bathroom and saw all the—"

"So you just slunk away like the coward you are," Arthur said, eyes narrowing.

"I didn't know what else to do!" Rob cried. "Oh god! I didn't kill anyone. You have to believe me!"

Arthur stepped away, arching his back as he took a deep sigh and smiled at Mary-Margaret..

"I think we're done here, MM."

"Indeed," Mary-Margaret said, looking at the cowering young man whimpering into his hands. "Ah, luv, perhaps Sister Augustine...ach, perhaps ye'd be best to pop into the lads' jacks just around the corner and freshen yerself up before ye leave."

Mary-Margaret opened the office door.The young man looked up at her and Arthur, and then bolted out of the room.

"Good cop, bad cop. I think we nailed it," Arthur said, pulling off the headpiece and flicking his head from side to side, as if he had enough hair that it would move at all.

Chapter Twenty-Four

"So are we all just havin' a lie-in today?" Mary-Margaret said, turning from the stove to see Michael walk into the kitchen.

"First time in a long time, Mom. Not at the church today?"

"Haven't received an urgent phone call from Father Miguel, beggin' me to come in, so I'm assumin' The New Girl is back."

"Any coffee made?"

"No, but I've just this minute turned the kettle on. I'll make ye a cuppa as well then, luv."

"I'd prefer coffee, Mom."

"I've got the kettle on now, so sitcheedoon out at the table and I'll get yer rollies ready for ye as well."

Michael nodded and went back out to the dining room.

"Is Max at school?" Michael called back.

"Drove him meself. I think it tickles him a wee bit when the other lads see him pullin' up in Daphne."

"It is an amazing car, Mom."

"Here ye go. Now eat. It'll do ye a world of good," Mary-Margaret said, plunking a bowl of oatmeal down in front of Michael and then added, "I'll get ye a spoon."

She returned with a spoon and sat down at the head of the table, just to Michael's left.

"Speakin' of Daphne, someone tried to break into her the other night at O'Leary's."

"This after someone tried to run you off the road? Do you think someone

131

might be trying to tell you something?" Michael said, digging into the porridge.

"I can't speak to me near-death experience, but I've no concerns regardin' the other."

"And why is that?" Michael said, his spoon suspended in mid-air as he awaited her answer.

"I spoke to the lad, and we're all good."

"What do you mean 'I spoke to the lad'?"

"We communicated with each other. We—"

"I know what *spoke* means, Mom. I'm just trying to envision this guy standing by your car after trying to—"

"Ach, Michael. Don't be daft. He didn't stick around."

"So, how did you end up speaking to him?"

"He left his card."

Michael stared at his mother, setting his spoon down.

"His library card. It's got his name on it. I called the library and got his phone number and—"

"They're not supposed to give out that information," Michael said, cocking his head to one side while squinting his eyes. "How did you—"

"The how matters not. The main thing is that I spoke to him yesterday afternoon at the Church. Lovely young lad. Just a bit misguided, is all."

"Aren't they all?" Michael commented, shaking his head as he picked up his spoon and took a large mouthful of porridge.

"Not all of them, Michael, but more than a few. Which ye'd know if ye came to church—"

"Speaking of the church, you said you thought the new secretary was back. Does that mean you're all done?"

"I believe so. Just as well, I'd say, since I've got this murder to keep me busy now."

"About that, Mom—"

"Our Mandy says working murders like she does makes her feel alive. I get that. Nothin' like starin' death in the face every day to make ye thank yer lucky stars."

"So now you and Mandy are pals?"

"Always were, Michael. She reminds me so much of meself, truth to be told."

"Is that so?" Michael took another spoonful of porridge.

"Absolutely. The world on her shoulders, and she walks like Danú herself. Ye know, she was thinkin' that me bein' involved as I am—"

"Not—" Michael said, his mouth full.

"Is likely a good thing. Said I had a real eye for this sort of thing."

"What sort of thing, Mom?"

"Death. Murder. Homicide. It takes a certain spirit to take it all in like me and Mandy do, ye know. That may be why ye are not in Homicide, Michael. Ye don't have the spirit for it."

"Something like that. How's your foot?"

"Me foot?"

"Yes," he said, poking at the remainder of his porridge before continuing. "You know, that thing at the bottom of your leg that you put a shoe on? That was broken?"

"Oh, me foot." Mary-Margaret waving her hand dismissively. "Well, funny thing, Michael. What with all of this church business and then Jane Ann, I've hardly had a moment to give it any thought. Which is just as well because I'm off to speak to Jane Ann's lad at the cookie factory this aft before—"

"What cookie factory?"

"Did I say cookie factory? I meant...I'm off to get some cookies. Yes. And I think I've left the stove on. Just a moment, luv."

She rose and left the table.

"And what's this about Jane Ann's lad?" Michael called after her.

"I canna hear ye," Mary-Margaret called back. "Scrubbin' the burn off the pot, dontcha know."

"How are you doing all of this with your broken foot?"

"I still canna hear ye," Mary-Margaret blasted the water out of the faucet.

"I don't know what's going on, and I don't think I want to know what's going on, but you seem a lot better," Michael said to no one in particular.

"Indeed. But not too better," Mary-Margaret called out from the kitchen.

"For what?"

"Goin' home," she said, trying her hands with a dish towel as she walked out of the kitchen.

"Who said anything about going home? I was just thinking that I've seen you more without your crutches than with them, and you seem to be doing just fine without them."

"And when have ye ever seen me without me crutches?"

"I saw some footage of the murder on the news and you were in the background. Seemed to be getting around quite well without—"

"On the news?" Mary-Margaret beamed. "On the telly? Ye saw me on the news on the telly, did ye?"

"Yep. And I was talking to Teaszy. She was saying something about—"

Mary-Margaret jumped up from her seat. "Ach, Michael, forgive me, me son. I've got a pot of tea steepin', and I'm just realizin' that it's past the five-minute mark. If I don't rescue it now, I'll be able to use it to fuel me car."

"Mom, your foot isn't broken, is it?"

"Michael..." Mary-Margaret stopped in the doorway and turned to look at him. "What exactly are ye sayin'?"

"I'm saying your foot isn't broken. Never was."

"And since when did ye become an orthopedic surgeon?" she said before falling into a fit of coughing.

"Are you all right,? Do you need a glass of water?" Michael got up and walked over to her.

"No, lad. It's just a wee cough. Had it for the past couple of days. Might be a bit of a bug. Might be a bit of the pneumonia setting in."

"Pneumonia?" Michael repeated.

"Well, at me age, luv, it all comes back to the pneumonia. Just a matter of time, me doctor says. Lucky if it isn't actually the death of me one day. But don't worry. I've got a place to be, back at me own house. And what with The New Girl being back, I've got nothin' to keep me occupied. Except for the pleas of me one friend's daughter—one murdered friend's daughter—to help find her mother's killer...."

Just then, Phil came bounding down the stairs.

"Ah, and I've got wee Phil," Mary-Margaret sighed, bending down to scratch the frenzied dog's ear as it darted past her towards the back door. "Don't suppose ye could let him out for a wee piddle, could ye, Michael, while I check our tea?"

Michael walked to the back door in the kitchen and opened it. The dog raced out.

"About that," he said, watching Phil run down the alley to the nearest fence and release an extraordinarily heavy stream of urine. "How long is Sally-next-door going to be away?"

"Don't trouble yerself about that, me son. I'll be on me way soon enough, and Phil will be out from under."

Phil ran back into the house and, as Michael expected, entangled himself in between Michael's legs.

"I'm worried about you, Mom."

"Don't be. At me age, ye learn to take care of yerself. Especially me, bein' on me own and all for so long..."

"No, I'm worried about you getting involved in this murder investigation. I told you last night that Homicide had a suspect and—"

"They've got nothin'," she interrupted.

"How do you know?"

"Mandy told me."

"Told you what?"

"Just what I said to ye, Michael. Ye know, perhaps it is I that should be worried about ye. Are ye havin' this much trouble followin' along at work as well, then?"

"I've known Amanda Black a very long time, and I can't imagine that she would be disclosing anything to anyone outside of the team about an ongoing homicide investigation. Are you sure you're not just imagining this?" Michael said, raising his voice.

"Did ye just call yer mam senile?" Mary-Margaret said, her head snapping back as if she'd been slapped in the face.

"No, but you have been known to...lose the thread...on the odd conversation."

"Never. 'Tis ye who has lost the thread. And, as ye've just said, Michael, I cannot disclose exactly what we spoke of because it's police business and all. But I can tell ye that she is of the opinion that the lad in charge of the investigation is swimmin' deep in the shallow end most of the time and might not be the one to solve this crime."

Michael stared at his mother.

"Well, those may not have been her exact words, but I know that's what she meant. Now if ye'll excuse me. Ye may have the mornin' off, but I've got to get meself over to Jane Ann's place."

Michael shook his head in a mix of despair, frustration, and disbelief.

"And before ye get sayin' what ye are thinkin', 'twas Chrystal who has asked me to help her clean the apartment."

"Please be careful, okay, Mom?"

"I shall, me son," Mary-Margaret assured him. "And one more thing."

"Do tell."

"I cannot tell a lie. Me foot isn't broken. Never was, never will be, God willin'."

"So why did you say it was?"

"Because ye needed me here. And if I didn't have a reason, ye would have sent me on me away, and God knows what mess ye would be in by now."

"So why didn't you just say that?"

"Because ye wouldn't have listened. I'll pack up me room when I get back from Jane Ann's and have Max take me home this evening."

"You don't have to, Mom."

"No. I have overstayed me welcome and am now just—" Mary-Margaret burst into another round of coughs.

"Sit down, Mom," Michael said, gently taking his mother by the arm and leading her to one of the chairs by the front window. "Are you sure you should be going out? Maybe you're pushing yourself too hard?"

"Horsefeathers! It's just a wee cough." She slumped into the chair. "'Tis unlikely this strain of the pneumonia is like that which almost killed yer Aunt Fionnuala a few years back. But she was always delicate, was our Fionnuala."

"Who is or was Aunt Fionnuala?"

"Me sister, Michael. Who else would she be?"

"You've never spoken of a sister named Fionnuala."

"Ye never asked. Now," she said firmly, getting up from the chair, "if I'm goin' I'm goin', and if I'm stayin', I'm stayin'. Which will it be?"

"Of course, you're staying, but—"

"Good. Right. So," she removed her purse from the hook by the front door. "Just so as ye know where we're at: I'll be pickin' Max up from after school. I don't expect that ye will be home for dinner—am I right or am I right?—so it will just be him and me. Unless somethin' turns up at Jane Ann's this afternoon. I'm off now to help Chrystal clear the place out. Or unless our lad...oh, never mind. In any event, unless somethin' turns up, I'll be home for the duration."

"What do you mean: 'unless something turns up'...? And what's this about 'our lad'?"

"Michael, correct me if I'm wrong, but ye are a police officer, are ye not? And so ye do know that not everythin' unfolds as it should in these types of things."

"Mom..."

"Michael, me tea! With all of yer thisin' and thatin', I've left it too long!" Mary-Margaret raced past Michael into the kitchen and then called back to him. "Oh, and one other thing: If ye see our Mandy, don't tell her what I told ye about our Billy Gilly lad and all, right?"

Once again, Michael shook his head in disbelief as he sat down in front of the bowl of cold porridge and, knowing that resistance was futile, took another spoonful.

Chapter Twenty-Five

As she walked into the cookie factory, Mary-Margaret was underwhelmed. But for the sugary smell, this place could just as easily have been entering the bowels of the Central Bank of Ireland. The gray cement floor and walls and the large security office to her left were nothing like Willy Wonka's Chocolate Factory that she had been expecting to see

"I'm sorry, ma'am, but this area is not open to the general public," the gangly security guard advised through a round shape made up of a series of tiny holes in the plexiglass, his voice and uniform seeming much too big for his body.

"Well," Mary-Margaret shot back, "that works out well for the both of us, doesn't it, lad, because I am not the general public."

"My apologies, ma'am," the young man said, pushing a clipboard with a pen through an opening at the bottom of the barrier towards her. "If you're here for the board meeting, it's being held in the other building. Please sign in, and I'll walk you through the tunnel."

Mary-Margaret thought for a moment, unsure about which annoyed her more: her disappointment with the banality of the cookie factory or that she could actually hear Father Miguel's words in her head about the sin of lying.

"No, I'm not here for that. I'm here to see Jerry LaMarshe," she said, hoping that the telling of a truth would give God the proof he needed to know that whatever else might follow, her aim was true.

"Who?"

"Jerry," Mary-Margaret repeated slowly. "La. Marshe. He works here."

"Oh. I see. Just a minute while I check employee records. Do you know what section he's in?"

"The cookie making section." Not the brightest light on the block, this lad, she thought.

The security guard stopped and looked squarely at the older woman standing on the other side of the barrier.

"Why do you want to see this employee?" he asked, eyes narrowing.

"I've business with him that is none of yours," Mary-Margaret said, straightening her back. Forgive me, Father, but I feel a slight fabrication might be in order.

"Really?"

"Well, truth to be told, lad," Mary-Margaret said, leaning towards the small round opening, "I've urgent news that can't wait, and I don't want to tell him over the phone."

The young man turned his head slightly.

"Are you his mother?"

"I beg your pardon?" Mary-Margaret said, stepping away from the plexiglass.

"I just thought, you know, the only two people who have that kind of news are your mother or your doctor?"

"And ye didn't think to first ask if I was the latter?" Mary-Margaret shot back, a new identity presenting itself to her. "Ye just assumed, because I'm a woman, that I had to be the lad's mam? Have ye never seen a woman doctor before, lad? Back in the day, it might not have been unusual to only have one or two women in medical school, but these days, lad. Ach. I thought we were all over that silly business."

"No, I-I-I," the young man struggled. "Do you have any ID?"

"ID? Like what? A driver's license? Of course," Mary-Margaret said, pressing her purse against the plexiglass as she snapped opened the clasp to pull out a wallet.

"No, I mean something that says you're a doctor."

"Well, I'm sorry, lad," she said sharply, snapping the clasp shut. "I've left me doctoring kit in me car. I can run out and get it, if that will satisfy ye?

If I wanted to pass this much time, I would have just rung up our Jerry, for whom time, as ye may recall, is critical."

The young man blushed.

"Now, are ye goin' to give him a ring and get him out here, or shall we just put Cause Of Death as...?"

The young man quickly looked back to the computer screen, scrolled down, and then picked up the receiver of the phone beside him.

"It's a good thing yer not a medic, lad. At the pace ye go, yer patient would have bled out," Mary-Margaret said just loud enough for the young man to hear.

"Have a seat, Doctor...?"

"O'Shea. O'Sheen," she corrected herself. Father, ye know me intentions are pure. No need to ask forgiveness. And if there is, we'll chat later. "Doctor Mary-Frances O'Sheen."

"Doctor O'Sheen. LaMarshe will be down in a moment."

"I hope so, lad. Time is not on his side."

"Would you like a room to wait in, Doctor?"

"Indeed. And I expect some privacy while I'm advisin' me patient of his condition."

"Ah, sure. Of course," the young man replied, grabbing at his belt to pull on a packed keychain as he took a step out of the office. "Come with me. I'll let you into this room down the hall."

"Is that goin' to be private enough, lad? I am goin' to be tellin' our Jerry some things that may be a bit...upsettin'."

"Right," the security guard said, moving back into the office, the keychain snapping back against his body with a loud jangle. He looked up at a wall of keys. "There's a really nice office here on the main floor that the national VP uses when she's here. Would that work?"

"Does this room have its own jacks?" Mary-Margaret asked, realizing that she could have done without that last cuppa before heading out.

The security guard froze, arm extended to pluck the key from its hook.

"Ye know: facilities. Loo. Washroom. The logic behind me request is too complicated for me mind to unravel to ye in this moment."

"Yes, of course it does."

"Excellent."

"No worries. And the back door of the factory is across from that office. It leads into the parking lot, which would be good if, you know, the news kind of...?"

"I see where ye are leadin' with this. If I need an ambulance or the police or anythin' like that, I can just call ye up here at the front, and they'll come 'round to where we are."

"Exactly," the security guard said, striding quickly down the hall, neglecting to get Mary-Margaret to sign in on his clipboard.

"I take it back, lad," she said, taking two steps to his one. "With a wee bit more trainin', ye might manage as a medic after all."

* * *

Mary-Margaret had just sat down behind the massive mahogany desk in perhaps the most comfortable chair she had ever known when the security guard returned with a man that didn't look much older than himself in tow.

"I'll leave you two," the guard said with a somber nod, showing Jerry LaMarshe in before closing the door behind him.

"Who are you?" he said, standing just inside the doorway.

"That's not what I'm here to talk about, Jerry," Mary-Margaret said with a blend of authority and compassion that she hoped would soften this potential killer up enough to talk to her. "Sitcheedon, lad."

Jerry sat in the chair across from her, not looking at all comfortable.

"When did ye last see Jane Ann Hill?"

"Are you a cop?"

"Do I look like a cop? Now, if I were ye, I'd answer the questions, and then we can both be on our way."

"Because if you're a cop, I want my car back."

"Answer me question first, and then we'll have a wee word about yer car."

"Ok. I saw her a couple of Sundays ago. Now, about my car?"

"When a couple of Sundays ago?"

141

"Morning, if you must know."

"Indeed. I must. Yer car has been seized, lad. I don't think this is a time for bein' clever."

"Ok. I stayed over Saturday night. Like I told your boys, that's what I usually did."

"Spent the night, then?" Mary-Margaret suppressed a smile. No wonder she stopped comin' to church.

"Yeah. Is that a crime?"

"Fair ball. So ye've told...me boys...all of this, then?"

"Yeah. Of course. So about my car?"

"Ye do know that yer lass is—"

"Dead? Yeah. I know. Your boys told me when they dragged me in to—what is it they say? Talk? And seized my car. They let me go, but not my car. So. How about it?"

"Ah, right. Not exactly the romantic type, are ye?"

"Apparently not."

"Well then," Mary-Margaret said, beginning to see why people would think this man might have killed Jane Ann. "Why do ye think they've still got yer car?"

"I dun—wait—did you say 'they'? So you're not a cop?"

"Did I say I was a cop? Stay close, lad. I've not got all day for this. Now, why is yer car not back to ye?"

"If you're not a cop, why are you here?"

"Let's keep the questions comin' from this side of the table, shall we?"

"It has nothing to do with Jane Ann, if that's what you're asking."

"What else would I be askin' about?"

"You're not a cookie cop, either?"

"Lad, I think ye've been breathin' in those sicky sweet dough fumes for a bit too long. Ye aren't makin' any sense at all."

"I thought you were part of the security company they have here."

"Oh, me stars. It's goin' from bad to worse!"

"So who are you?"

"It doesn't matter. Tell me about the car."

"Are you the lawyer the union sent?"

"Well—"

"Because if you are, it wasn't my idea."

"What wasn't?"

"We're done," Jerry said, getting up from the chair. "But just so you know, they won't find what they're looking for in my car."

"And why is that, lad?"

"Because I was careful. Very careful."

Chapter Twenty-Six

"Are ye alright in there, luv?" Mary-Margaret called out as she opened the unlocked door to Jane Ann's apartment.

"Yikes, you startled me," Chrystal said, poking her head around the bathroom door.

"Ach, ye had to get in there, did ye?"

"Figured I'd start with the worst."

"Time for a cuppa, then. I've got some news of me own. Where might the kettle be?" Mary-Margaret looked around the kitchenette for the kettle.

"Bottom right. Beside the stove."

"Ta, luv." Mary-Margaret pulled the kettle out and filled it with water.

"You said you had news."

"Indeed. How well did ye know Jerry LaMarshe?"

"Not well, why?"

"Well, I had a wee word with our lad just now."

"And?"

"I wouldn't be takin' a pint with him in the pub, that much I can say."

"Do you think...?"

"Thinkin' is for the likes of the media woman, Janelle Austin. We need to know."

"Sorry?"

"What I'm sayin' is we need proof."

"What about his car?"

"Seemed a bit too excited about gettin' his car back for my likin', but that doesn't make him a murderer. Although...." Mary-Margaret said, plugging in the kettle.

Chrystal waited for Mary-Margaret to continue, but the older woman did not.

"Although what?"

"He said somethin' about bein' careful. Rubbed me the wrong way, did that. He's guilty—"

"So you do think he murdered my mother?"

"Not necessarily, but I do think he's guilty of somethin'. I'll have to have another word with him. In the meantime, have ye spoken with the police?"

"Not since I gave them my statement. Why?"

"No reason. Just wonderin'." She rooted through the cupboards above the stove. "Now, if I were sugar, where would I be?"

"You wouldn't. Mom never had any sugar."

Horrified, Mary-Margaret froze.

"I know. She had a thing about sugar. Thought it caused cancer." Chrystal came out of the bathroom, peeling the yellow rubber gloves off her hands and wiping her brow.

"Me cousin, Riona, thought it was cow's milk that caused it. Cursed every Dexter she passed. Odd ducks, aren't we? Never mind, then. Here, give me those gloves, luv. Garbage under the sink, I assume?" She opened the lower cupboard, but it was bare.

"Apparently not. Did your mam have an aversion to that, as well?"

"What? Oh, right. They must have taken it as evidence."

"Likely. I just hope they haven't taken the tea bags, too."

"It's hard to believe that my mom's place was a crime scene," Chrystal said, collapsing on the couch. "I haven't even thought about her being dead yet."

Mary-Margaret joined her. "Ach, luv. It's a long road, this one is. I remember when me Jimmy died, God rest his soul. Took me months before I took the pillowcase off his pillow. The girls had taken to sleeping in bed with me after he was gone. Wouldn't let them touch his pillow. Thought I was daft, I'm sure, but it smelled like him. Felt like him. Reminded me that he had actually been there as the world carried on without him."

Both women sat looking at nothing. The kettle boiled and a click could be heard as it shut itself off.

"And then one day, I pulled the pillowcase off and threw it in the machine. Which is to say, me luv, that life goes on and so do we. Now, let me see about that cuppa." She walked back to the kitchenette to make the tea. "No tea pot, I see. Well, never mind."

"I know in my head that things will get better, but—"

"Things do get better. Now, have ye got a box for yer keepsakes? Ye can't take everythin' with ye, and I would suggest ye sort out what ye actually want and what we can just take out when we go. Have ye spoken to Nancy yet? We're gettin' close to the end of the month, and ye don't want to be payin' for a place ye don't have need for, so we either have to put on the jets or see about her lettin' us have an extra few days."

"No wonder my mother liked you, Mary-Margaret. You're so practical."

"Well, I wouldn't say that, but I would say that the clock is tickin', and we…you…have a lot to do. Is the funeral planned, then?"

"I haven't even—"

"No mind. I'll look after it, if ye like. I can ring Father Miguel later this aft and see when he's available. Has her body been released from the morgue yet?"

Chrystal erupted in a torrent of tears as Mary-Margaret held her, stroking her back.

"Ach, luv," Mary-Margaret said, coming around the counter to sit beside Chrystal. "There's me bein' all…practical. Here, give us a hug, then. That's it, luv. Let it out. Let it out. This is likely one of the hardest days of yer life. And then there's the funeral. But we'll all be there with ye to give her a good sendoff. I'll make sure of that. Now, let's have that cuppa and think for a moment. The police haven't spoken to ye again, ye say?"

"They've ruled me out as a suspect, if that's what you're asking," Chrystal said, wiping her tears from a tissue she'd pulled from her pocket. "They took one look at Mom's finances and saw that I had nothing to gain there. And then, when I told them about how we were just starting to get to know each other again."

She broke down into another round of sobs.

"It's all right, luv," Mary-Margaret said, giving Chrystal another hug.

The two women sat quietly on the couch together for a few minutes, Chrystal's sobs turning into whimpers, turning into the occasional sniffle.

When she thought Chrystal was calmed down enough, Mary-Margaret brought out the tea. "Here ye go, luv. So now, let's focus our thoughts on somethin' we can do."

"Like what?" Chrystal asked, looking lost amongst her deceased mother's belongings.

"Find out who did this to yer mam."

"Well, the police did ask if there was anyone I could think of who might want to hurt Mom, but aside from Jerry—"

"So ye do think he'd want to harm her."

"No. It's just, you know, that's how it always is on TV." Chrystal laughed.

"Ach, if only life was like it was on the telly. We'd all be taller, thinner, and richer."

"Do you know of anyone who would want to kill my mother, Mary-Margaret?"

"And how would I be knowin' that, luv?" she said, getting up to look around the apartment. "Now, I'm lookin' at this closet here." She moved a big garbage bag away from a door that opened into a walk-in closet in the corner of the living room, "and thinkin' that this would be the place to start cleaning out. Oh, my."

"What is it?"

"Nothin', I'm sure, luv," she said, looking up at the twenty or so boxes piled high behind the door. "I just didn't expect so many boxes."

"Mom held on to a lot of things, I suppose."

"I'm seein' if the labels mean anythin', that most of what she held onto was yours."

"What do you mean?" Chrystal asked, walking over to the closet.

"School Photos K-G13, Baptism/First Comm, Artwork K-6," Mary-Margaret started to read the labels clearly written on the boxes. "I don't suppose these could be anyone else's but yours."

"Wow. I had no idea."

"Ach, what's this, then?" Mary-Margaret pointed to a box closer to the back that was not stacked neatly like all the rest, making it look quite out of place in the otherwise orderly closet.

"Here. Let me just move these boxes in front and—"

"I'll pull them out, Mary-Margaret. Hang on a minute."

Chrystal pulled out more than a dozen sealed banker's boxes before she could reach the one in question.

"Is this the box you mean?" She pulled out the only box that was not taped shut.

"Indeed." Mary-Margaret motioned for Chrystal to set the box down on the floor by the couch. "Confirmation. If yer da lived in this parish, then ye were confirmed at St. Francis."

"Yes, I was, although I don't ever recall my father coming to church. I don't recall ever seeing my mother there, either. She was long gone by the time I was confirmed, as far as I know. I can't imagine what she would have from my confirmation, or why it would take up a whole box."

"Nor can I, but," Mary-Margaret said, taking off the box lid, "here's your dress. Not folded very well. More like stuffed in, I'd say."

"How would she get that?"

"From yer da? And here's a photo album." Mary-Margaret passed it over to Chrystal. "And yer Exemplary Attendance medal. And they said no one keeps these."

"Where's my crucifix?" Chrystal said.

"Do ye remember that?" Mary-Margaret said with some satisfaction.

"Of course. It was the coolest thing back then."

"Back then?"

"You know what I mean. But it isn't here."

"Why wouldn't ye have it, if ye were livin' with yer da at the time?"

"I only wore it for a bit and then put it away."

"So ye would have it then."

"I remember leaving the crucifix and chain in my bedroom somewhere. I didn't think about it again until I went through my Madonna phase," Chrystal said.

"The singer?"

Chrystal nodded slightly.

"And then I couldn't find it anywhere."

"Yer da must have packed it up and given it to yer mam with all of yer other things."

"I just find that so odd. I mean, I didn't even think he knew where she was, never mind that he actually gave her my stuff."

"Clearly he did."

"He must have really loved her."

"He loved ye, I would say."

"So where is the crucifix? Maybe it's in another box," Chrystal said, looking at the labels of the remaining boxes. "Or maybe my dad never gave it to her, or maybe—"

"Someone took it. Recently."

"But who?"

"I don't know, luv. Someone who wanted somethin' of yer's."

"Aside from Jerry, there was no one—"

"That ye know of."

"That I know of," Chrystal conceded.

"Do you think the police might have taken it as evidence? I'm kind of surprised that they didn't take all of these boxes, to be honest. Don't they usually do that? Take everything, I mean?"

"You'd think, indeed. Although," Mary-Margaret sighed, "we are dealin' with Billy Gilly."

Chapter Twenty-Seven

Mary-Margaret's car did not have a radio in it. It was an added feature that Jimmy had thought was an unnecessary expense when he bought the car. As a result, Mary-Margaret usually sang at the top of her lungs. She often wondered, back when she was sitting beside him, belting out whatever tune came to her mind, how many times Jimmy had wished he had spent the extra few dollars.

After he passed and Mary-Margaret learned how to drive, she continued to sing at the top of her lungs. Any pop song from the eighties would do. Except for today. Coming home from Jane Ann's, she was silent.

She let herself in the back door of Michael's house after squeezing her car into the tiny spot off the alley that the real estate agents for the area were now using as a selling feature, referring to them 'a legal single car parking space.'

"Ach, Phil, have ye been alone all day, then?" she said as the tiny Jack Russell came charging at her. She reached for the leash hooked on the back of the door. "Might as well be back with Sally-next-door if this is the way it's going to be, eh, me lad? Here, let me take ye for a wee walk down the laneway. It's the least I can do."

"Still at Michael's, are you?" Doug, one of the neighbors standing with two other men in the alleyway, said, gesturing with a full glass of wine.

"Sure enough," Mary-Margaret answered.

"I don't mean it like that, but when are you going home?" Charles asked, pouring himself a glass of wine from the bottle by his foot.

"And how do ye mean it, then?" Mary-Margaret shot back harshly. The notion of grown men standing behind their houses in a laneway in the early evening drinking like this did not sit well with her at all.

"What he's trying to say," Johnny, a small man who was always unshaven said as he took a swig of beer from a can, "is how long is Michael going to have his mommy taking care of him?"

They all laughed.

"As long as need be. As if it be any business of yers, then."

Mary-Margaret would have walked right past the group, except Phil chose this moment to release his bowels. With as much decorum as she could muster, Mary-Margaret reached down with a plastic bag that had been tied to the leash and picked up the poop.

"Is Mike involved in this latest homicide at all?" Doug asked.

"Which homicide would that be?" Mary-Margaret asked, taking a moment to notice that these men were not that much younger than she was.

"The one where they just made an arrest. It's been all over the news," Charles said. "We thought Mike might be involved somehow."

"Well, if they've made an arrest, ye can be sure me Michael was involved. Now, if ye don't mind..."

"It's the drugs, isn't it," Doug asked.

"What is?" Mary-Margaret replied.

"That makes them do it. Back in our day, booze and lust made them do it. These days, it's drugs. Or guns. This kid can't be more than twenty-one or twenty-two—"

"Twenty-three. They say they've got some video footage where they see him leaving the old girl's apartment," Charles said, pulling out his iPhone to check for the latest updates.

"Old girl? Which homicide are we talkin' about, lads?"

"The one from the co-op, where they found her body in the ravine nearby."

"From the co-op?" Mary-Margaret echoed.

"Terrible thing, these drugs," Doug continued. "Remember, Charles—well, you may not, but you will, Johnny—when we used to share a joint between us and think that was a big thing? Now these kids are doing—"

"Oh, I've had my share of marijuana back in the day," Charles protested, looking up from the screen.

"Give us a look, then," Mary-Margaret said, forgetting about Phil as she walked over to Charles.

"Here. Top story. Cops pulled him from a bus a couple of hours ago."

"Me eyes are not what they were. Here," Mary-Margaret said, grabbing the phone away from Charles.

"How do ye work this thing? Scroll up here?" she asked, madly rubbing the screen.

"Like this," Charles said, cautiously retrieving his phone, then holding it down for Mary-Margaret to see as he scrolled through the story while she quietly read it aloud.

"'Found the body in a ravine,'" Johnny echoed. "That's gotta be a messed-up sight."

"And that's why I don't have a dog," Charles said, pulling his iPhone back from Mary-Margaret.

"That makes no sense," Johnny said.

"I imagine it was a dog walker who found the body, wouldn't you think? I mean, who else goes near a ravine?"

"Some dude dumping a body," Johnny laughed.

"Anything wrong, Mary-Margaret?" Doug asked.

"No, not at all. Well, enjoy yer wine and tinnies."

"We're out every evening. Feel free to join us," Charles said, wiping off the iPhone before putting it back in his pants pocket.

"It shall be a frosty Tuesday before ye see the likes of me out here with ye," she said coldly as she pulled Phil back into Michael's house. "Imagine, me, out back in a laneway with a gang of lads as old as I, practically drinkin' from a bottle. Frosty Tuesday indeed."

She hurriedly unclipped the leash from the dog's collar while he stood expectantly at her feet.

"What now?"

Phil looked up at her, tail wagging.

"Ach, wee Phil, I've got to get the telly on first, and then I'll get ye yer bicky."

Phil barked at her before following her into the living room.

"That's right, Greg," reporter Janelle Austin was saying as Mary-Margaret finished fumbling with the numerous remote controls required to turn on the TV. "Police now have twenty-three-year-old Robert Davis Jackson in custody for the murder of Jane Ann Hill. I've spoken to Detective William Gill, who advises that Jackson will be held in custody overnight before appearing right here in Old City Hall Courts tomorrow morning."

"And do they expect that he'll get bail, given the randomness and brutality of this particular murder, Janelle?"

"Hard to say, Greg," Janelle said, walking slowly down the stone steps of the courthouse towards the camera, a uniformed officer talking to a woman in a suit ducking past her. "As you've so rightly stated, this was a seemingly senseless attack on an elderly woman—"

"Elderly, me ear!" Mary-Margaret snapped.

"…that has left the community feeling quite afraid."

"Afraid, yes, but now that they have the murderer—"

"Alleged murderer, Greg."

"Alleged murderer in custody, are there any other concerns about having this man roam free in the neighborhood?"

"Well, Greg, that has yet to be seen. Police are unusually tight-lipped about this one."

"What do you mean by 'unusually tight-lipped,' Janelle?"

"They have not given us much information about the accused, Greg. As you know, there would usually have been a press conference of some sort after an arrest like this, but not," Janelle paused for a moment before concluding with, "today."

"You've been covering the crime beat for a very long time, Janelle. Any ideas why this might be the case?"

"Indeed, Greg, I have. And while it may not be the case here, it has been my experience that the police are tight-lipped when they have something they don't want made public."

"Ha!" Mary-Margaret sneered. "Thanks for that scrap of genius, ye silly sausage. After all these years, Janelle, ye still don't now yer head from yer arse."

"Like what?"

"Well, Greg, it's hard to say. Maybe they have some hold-back information—"

A mugshot of the accused flashed on the screen. Mary-Margaret did not hear the rest of what the reporter said.

"That's Bobbo." she called out. "Our lad from the other day. That's not the murderer. Ye've got the wrong lad."

Mary-Margaret clicked off the TV while Phil's entire body wagged at her feet.

"Ach, Phil, what is this world comin' to? They think Bobbo's a murderer. A lad that wees himself in front of a nun is just not capable of gougin' a woman to death the way Jane Ann was. I've got to call someone. Me Michael. Yes. I'll call me Michael. Once I get the breath back into me. How about we get ye yer bicky, then."

The dog wagged himself even harder.

"Well, so be it. Come along then to the kitchen. I'll get me phone and call me Michael. It was lust, not drugs, that drove the killer, and Bobbo is certainly not a lusty lad. Oh, I know what yer thinkin', Phil. They look at me now and wonder what can she know about the ways of men, but I wasn't always the mother of me children or Mrs. O'Shea from the Church."

Mary-Margaret pulled a sealed bag of dog treats from the cupboard under the counter and hand-fed Phil three of them.

"That's enough for now, wee Phil. With the lack of exercise ye have been gettin' as of late and the increase in treats, ye will not be wee much longer. Now, where is me cell phone?"

Mary-Margaret looked around the kitchen to no avail. Phil just continued to look hopeful.

"Ach, I've left it in me car. Good thing they've got the wrong man. Otherwise, I'd have forgotten all about me purse, and me window would be smashed and the purse gone, sure as there is iron in Guinness."

* * *

"Hello, can ye page Detective Michael O'Shea, please? No...Don't transfer me back. He's not pickin' up the line. He's probably in the jacks... Yes, and tell him over the loudspeaker that it's his mam. Ta, luv."

She waited a few minutes, listening to the classical music playing in her ear.

"Hi, Mom," Michael said.

"Hello, son. 'Tis yer mam."

"Yes, I know. And so does everyone in the station. What can I do for you?"

"It's about Bobbo."

"Who?"

"The Jackson lad. The young fella they've arrested for Jane Ann's murder."

"I have no idea what you're talking about."

"Bobbo. The lad. It was on the news. Ach, Michael! Listen. They've got the wrong lad."

"Saints preserve us," Michael said in his thickest brogue. "Are me ears playin' tricks on me? Have me senses been seized by the wee people?"

"Michael!"

"Come on, Mom. Since when do you listen to what Janelle Austin has to say, and even if you do, since when do I listen to what she has to say?"

"Michael. I'm tellin' ye: he's the wrong lad."

"And how do you know this, Mom."

"Because he told me so."

"Of course he did."

"Ach, Michael, if ye won't believe yer mam, and what a sorry day in this mortal world that would be, do us a favor and answer me this: is your Mr. Jackson right- or left-handed?"

"How am I supposed to know, and even if I did, I can't tell you that."

"Ye would know if ye checked yer computer, and ye would tell me because I'm yer mam."

"He wasn't booked in here, Mom, and I couldn't tell you even if you were my mother."

"I am yer mam, lad. And I am seriously worried about yer bein' back at work so soon after that head-bashin'."

"It was a shoulder dislocation this time, Mom."

"Well, at least ye know who ye are talkin' to at the moment. Regardless, it seems to be affecting yer head. Now before ye lapse into a coma, find out if our Bobbo is right- or left-handed."

"Mom—"

"Michael, I would be callin' Mandy, but I don't have her cell phone number programmed in me phone."

"You wouldn't, and you do."

"Ye are talkin' gibberish, Michael."

"You wouldn't be calling Detective Black and I know you do have her cell number and her home number and every other bit of contact information for her programmed into your phone."

"That's neither here nor there, son, and we're wastin' time. Right- or left-handed?"

There was a long pause.

"Michael? Are ye there, lad? Ye haven't gone into a coma, have ye?"

"No, I haven't. I'm just in a state of... So why do you care if he's right- or left-handed?"

"Because it matters."

"Why? Don't tell me he's your sister Clementine's son, and you're trying to figure out who to sit him beside at our next Sunday dinner."

"Don't be daft, lad. I don't have a sister named Clementine. Honestly, luv. I worry about ye. All I'm tryin' to figure out now is if he was the one who stabbed Jane Ann fourteen times or not."

There was an even longer pause.

"How do you know that?" Michael said sternly.

"Know what, luv?"

"How many times she was stabbed."

"Because I do. Now—"

"No, Mom. How do you know that?"

"Because Francis told me. And he also told me that the murderer had to be left-handed. That's how. Are ye satisfied now? I've given ye my information, now give me yers."

"This isn't show-and-tell, Mom. And Frank could be in serious trouble."

"Well, he's not, is he, because no one knows anythin', do they? Except ye and me. And no one is going to be questioning me about it, are they? So now that ye know, ye have to do somethin' about it because ye are a policeman. Where ye got yer intel from—"

"Are you blackmailing me, Mom?"

"Ach, ye have been watchin' too many of those spy films, Michael. I'm tryin' to help ye out. This could be a murderer ye have caught without gettin' yer head bashed in. Go and check now!"

"Just a minute," Michael sighed, putting his mother on hold.

"Phil, I do worry about our Michael," Mary-Margaret said as classical music played in her ear again. "Such a clever lad at some things, and yet so dim at—"

"He's left-handed, Mom."

"What?"

"He's the one."

"B-but..."

"Mom, I know you thought you were going to save the day, but not this day."

"But did ye look at his face?"

"Doesn't look like a murderer? They don't always. I think we're done, Mom."

"Ach, no! No scrapes or scratches. No defence wounds. Francis told me Jane Ann put up a real fight. Under her nails—but Bobbo's face is as smooth as a baby's bottom."

"Bobbo?"

"Never mind. The logic behind it is too complicated for me mind to unravel to ye in this moment."

"I can only imagine," Michael said with a sigh.

"Ye need to do somethin' to free Bobbo."

"Like what?"

"Ye are askin' me?"

"No, Mom. What I'm really thinking is that Homicide likely has a whole

157

lot more evidence than you or I do, which is why they charged this guy."

"You have to find out who the real murderer is. And did ye have a look at the size of Bobbo? Even on the telly, Michael. Honestly. Do ye truly believe he could have dragged Jane Ann's body from her apartment into a car and then haul it out again and dump it in the ravine where it was found? We're talkin' about a lad who wee'd himself when Arthur—"

"Arthur spoke to him?"

"He was dressed as a nun at the time, so I'm not sure if that counts. Regardless, Bobbo is lucky to be able to haul his own bones around, let alone—"

"Mom, you've been told many times to stay away. You've even been cautioned for obstructing the police. And now I know that you've received information from the pathologist's technician. And you've spoken to one of the prior suspects."

"Two of them," she corrected.

"You have put me in a really awkward position, Mom. I am going to have to—"

"Sorry, luv. Phil is howlin' like a banshee. I'll let ye go, and we can talk later. And I'm sorry if ye feel ye are in a tight spot. Ye will get out of it, I'm sure. Bye-bye bye bye-bye-bye ."

Chapter Twenty-Eight

Mary-Margaret had not slept a wink, and it showed on the face that looked back at her from the mirror over the dresser in Michael's guest bedroom.

"Ach, take a look at ye, Mary-Margaret. Was a time when ye could work all the day long, go out to a pub and meet up with the gang, and sing and dance until dawn."

She looked down at Phil, his stump of a tail wagging madly, by her feet.

"Who am I kiddin', Phil? I'm gettin' as old as the rest of them, aren't I? No bother. Let's get ye out to the jacks."

As she wandered down the hall to the bathroom, she noticed Michael's bedroom door open and the drapes pulled back.

"What time is it, then?" Curious, she turned back to 'her' room to pick up her watch.

"Eleven thirty?" she squawked. "And no one had the decency to wake me to see if I was dead or alive? Ach, no wonder ye are chompin' at the bit, pup. Ye must be about ready to explode. Here, let me run ye out back, and then we'll have our cuppa and go for a proper walk to see what we can see that will help free our Bobbo."

She turned the heat up on the stove under the kettle, then waited at the back door for the few minutes it took Phil to find just the place to have a herculean pee. Then the two went back upstairs where Mary-Margaret got dressed for the day.

"Where's me cream? Might as well put on me face, Phil. Ye never know who ye will meet, as me dear old mam used to say. Might be a prince in frog's gear just waitin' for ye, she would say. I don't know which one of us girls she was thinkin' of when she said it, but I must have heard it backwards. At least until Jimmy, God rest his soul, came along. Ach, Phil, don't grow old, pup. Everyone dies."

She looked closely at her face in the mirror as she applied her lipstick and then, sighing, stepped back. "I don't know who this ancient girl in the mirror is who's lookin' back at me, Phil, but she surely isn't Mary-Margaret Donaghy."

The kettle whistled in the kitchen, setting the little dog to barking.

"Comin'," Mary-Margaret called out. "And ye, wee Phil: we'd best be off before the day gets away from us altogether."

Phil sat at her feet as she made a pot of tea, and then, looking at the time, rummaged through a kitchen cupboard for a travel mug. Having found one, she filled it with tea and made herself a jam sandwich.

"Hardly Belleek, but I'm sure it will do. Now let's get ourselves gone."

* * *

Twenty minutes later, they were at their destination: the wooded ravine about five minutes' drive from Jane Ann's co-op. As soon as Mary-Margaret opened Daphne's door, Phil was gone. Mary-Margaret, on the other hand, took her time as she stepped onto the path leading down into the ravine.

"The killer must have come this way," she said, walking along the path. Beyond the gate led down to a wooded area and a stream that was no more than a trickle in the summer, ideal for both dogs and young people to run wild. There were houses on either side of the street, but the occupants would be used to dog walkers during the day and groups of teens looking for a place to drink and make out late at night, everyone parking their cars where Mary-Margaret had parked hers. There was a sign that read, *No Parking 11:00 PM - 6:00 AM*, but parking rules were seldom enforced.

If the killer had driven to this exact spot, he would have had to drag Jane Ann's body only a few feet to the gate before he and his victim would be hidden from view.

Mary-Margaret pushed the overgrown branches away from her as she considered how to safely negotiate the path down to the stream. Hardened from years of walkers, the narrow path was still a bit precarious in spots where tree roots had pushed through, or the clay soil had eroded. So, while it was not difficult to follow, one could, if one was not careful, trip or slip off the path down into the stream.

With relative care, though, one could easily walk down into the heavily wooded area, past a few clearings showing signs of illicit merrymaking, to the bottom of the hill. Once there, it was a skip or a jump, depending on the season, to cross the stream, where the ravine opened up into a long-grassed field that eventually came to a road. One could easily walk for hours, crisscrossing the paths inside the wooded area without being seen.

As she made her way down towards the stream where Jane Ann's body had been found, Mary-Margaret wondered how much of the bushes and undergrowth had been trampled by the forensics officers and the media that fed off them. She wondered, too, how much the concentration of so many people and so much noise had impacted the routines of the ravine regulars: the squirrels, the raccoons, the chipmunks, the usual dog walkers, and the homeless people who found refuge here.

Clearly, routines had been disrupted because Mary-Margaret seemed to be the only person in the ravine, while Phil seemed to be the only dog. Luckily, there was an abundance of squirrels for him to chase.

Once she got to the stream, Mary-Margaret stopped.

Was this where Jane Ann's fully clothed body had been found, face down in the water?

I can't imagine what...? Put it out of yer mind, Mary-Margaret. Ye'll only be givin' yerself—

Suddenly, Phil appeared, tail wagging furiously, something in his mouth.

"Oh, for the love of God, Phil. Don't tell me ye've caught a rat."

The dog bounded towards her, shaking his head as he ran.

"Sweet Jesus, Mary, and Jose—" Her mouth dropped open.

The dog ran around her a couple of times, still shaking the bloody object in his mouth.

"Drop it," Mary-Margaret commanded. "Drop. It."

Phil stopped, sat down, and obediently dropped the object.

In spite of herself, Mary-Margaret trembled as she looked down at what the dog had found.

A bloody glove.

She reached into her jacket pocket and pulled out her cell phone. With shaking fingers, she hammered in the numbers.

"Detec—"

"Michael. This is yer mam."

"Hello, Mom," Michael sighed.

"Listen to me, son. I'm in the ravine by Jane Ann's, and wee Phil has found some evidence for her murder."

"Pardon?"

"I said—"

"I heard what you said, Mom. But what are you talking about?"

"Ach, Michael. Whatever it is ye are doin', ye need to stop it. I'm by the stream where ye found the body, and wee Phil has picked up a bloody glove."

"Mom, the forensics guys went up and down that stream a million times—"

"And wee Phil was up and down it once and found the murderer's glove. Grand. Yer lads missed it. Why? Because they did. Ye have told me yerself more than one story of key evidence turnin' up in the most unusual of ways. In any event, I don't know where wee Phil found it, but I've got it here. Now, if ye want to meet me here, ye can seize the glove and bring it in. Ye'll be Police Officer of the Year, Michael!"

"Hardly," Michael sighed. "How about you wait there and I'll have a uniformed—"

"Michael, they have had their shot at this. Now it's time for the pros—"

"You mean you?"

"I mean you. Get yerself down here, and we'll be away."

"Mom," Michael said, his voice becoming very serious. "Listen carefully to me. Stay right where you are. Do you have the glove with you?"

"Ach, Michael. That's what I've been tellin' ye!"

"Have you touched it?"

"And why would I?"

"Great. Don't. And keep the dog away from it. I'm having an officer come and see you. Don't move."

Before she could reply, Michael cut the connection.

"As if I've got nothin' else to do today but wait for a policeman to show up. Who does he think he is, Phil?"

Mary-Margaret looked around her for a moment before pulling a vanilla-scented bag from her jacket pocket.

"I don't suppose ye are required to scoop the poop here in the woods, so let's just put the glove in this bag, and we'll take it over to Mandy. She'll know what to do with it."

With that, she turned the bag inside out and, carefully putting it on her hand, picked up the glove.

* * *

"You have the glove, don't you, Mom?"

"To whom am I speaking, please?" Mary-Margaret replied, balancing her cell phone between her left shoulder and her ear as she got herself and the Jack Russell settled into her car.

"Where are you, Mom?"

"I'm in me car, luv. Where else would I be?"

"And you have the glove?"

"Of course I do."

"But I told you to—"

"I had to leave. The day gets busy when yer family leaves ye in yer bed until noon, likely thinkin' yer dead."

Michael sighed.

"Mom, you are interfering with a homicide investigation."

"It's some investigation when an old lady walkin' her dog finds key evidence. Maybe it's Janelle Austin I should be callin'."

"Okay, Mom. Where do you want me to meet you?"

"Well, I'm just about to take Phil home. Poor thing," she said, looking over her shoulder at the snoring dog sprawled out on the back seat of the car, "has quite knackered himself out. But lookin' at me watch, I'm thinkin' a good lunch at O'Leary's would be in order."

"How about you meet me at the station?"

"The police station? Not a chance. I'll perish before then. In fact, I can feel meself wastin' away as our gums are flappin' here and now."

"Mom, this is serious business."

"Ach. Me phone. It's runnin' out of interception."

"It can't run out of interception," Michael said, not trying to hide his annoyance.

"It's runnin' out of somethin'. Likely won't even make it to when I get to O'Leary's in about an hour."

"Mom—"

"Is that ye, Michael? I can't hear ye, luv. Ye are breakin'—"

"I am not breaking—"

"I can't hear ye. Michael? Michael? Ach, he's gone, Phil. I'm hoping' he knows enough to meet me at O'Learly's Pub in an hour." She kept talking into the cell phone, shouting the last five words. "And if he gets there before me, orders me a half-crown float. All of this business has quite upset me."

"Mom, I can hear you. And I'm not meeting you at O'Leary's. I'll meet you at home—"

"Terrible thing, these cell phones, Phil. We think they'll work all the time, but they don't. Ach, the line must be dead. Might as well hang up now—"

"I'm going to check on a few things here, and then I'll see you at home, Mom," Michael shouted from his end.

Chapter Twenty-Nine

"Not on my floors!" Arthur shouted, turning from the kitchen counter he was wiping and pulling his earbuds out as Phil bound through the back door.

"Ach, luv. I forgot ye'd be here today," Mary-Margaret said with a slight start.

"And what has happened to you?" Arthur asked as he led Mary-Margaret through the kitchen to her usual chair at the head of the dining room table. "Here, sit. Let me put on the kettle for you."

"Lookin' like the wrath of God, am I?"

"And then some. Girl, what have you been up to?"

"What's that noise I'm hearin'?"

"Motown. It's from my earbuds. Best music to clean to."

"I see. Well, I'll take that cuppa if ye'll join me."

"I am so behind—"

"This is important. Sitcheedoon while the kettle boils. I've got somethin' to tell ye."

"Hold that thought, MM." Arthur scooted back to the kitchen and, moving with surprising agility, started to put together the tea tray. "A biscuit with your tea?" Arthur popped his head back into the dining room, one earbud dangling, the other still in his ear. "I picked some up."

"Ach, ye are a lamb," Mary-Margaret said with a smile and then, under her breath, "And ye are certainly the proof in the pudding that the Lord works in mysterious ways."

"What was that, MM?"

"Nothin', luv. Just mutterin' away to wee Phil." She reached into her coat pocket to pull out the bag with the bloody glove.

"Now," Arthur said, bringing in a silver tray with two cups and saucers, a teapot, and a plate of cookies. Just as he began to pour the tea, he spotted the bag. "Why is that poo bag on my clean table?"

"Aren't we all posh today? Sitcheedoon, Arthur, and I'll explain it all to ye." Arthur dropped into the chair to her right.

"Are ye still plannin' on havin' a cuppa, though, Arthur?"

Arthur poured the tea, then leaned in towards Mary-Margaret, elbows on the table.

For the next fifteen minutes, Mary-Margaret told Arthur everything she knew about Jane Ann's murder. And the glove.

"And this...?"

"Is the glove," Mary-Margaret said, picking up the plastic bag by one corner and loosening the knot she had tied at the top of it.

"Don't, MM."

"And why not?"

"This is evidence, and we have to be careful with it."

Arthur removed the remaining earbud from his ear.

"Do you mean to tell me that ye have been listenin' to Etta James the whole time I was tellin' ye this story?"

"Absolutely not. She was never signed with Motown. She started with Modern and then signed to Chess—"

"And we need to discuss this now because?"

"I'm just saying, MM. I was actually listening to—"

"Me, I hope?"

"Uh, yes. Absolutely. Anyway, I think we should discuss the glove before we hand it over to the police. You say that Forensics had been all over that ravine, right?"

"Right."

"And yet they didn't find the glove."

"Apparently not."

"So, how do we know that this glove has anything to do with the murder?"

"And what else might it have to do with?"

"Well, I'm just saying that we can't go at this investigation with tunnel vision."

"Tunnel what?"

"Tunnel vision. You know, focusing on one thing to the exclusion of everything else. When is Michael coming to get the glove?"

"Any moment now," said Mary-Margaret.

"Then I'd better go." Arthur scooped up the bagged glove and headed out the back door.

"Where are you off to then?"

"The less you know, the better. But, buy me some time with Michael."

* * *

"Mom?"

"I'm up in the jacks, luv!" Mary-Margaret called down.

"Great. I haven't got much time. Where's this glove?"

"Can ye give a girl a moment?" Mary-Margaret adjusted herself before heading back downstairs.

"This is one of the worst things you have ever done," Michael said from the front doorway.

"Oh, I hardly think so."

"I don't have time for this, Mom. Where is the glove?"

"It's right...." She made a grand gesture towards the dining room table and then stopped, pulling both of her hands up to her mouth. "It's gone."

"You're kidding me, right?"

"Ach, lad. Arthur must have—"

"Oh no, Mom," Michael moaned, his shoulders slumping.

"Ach, it's not so bad, luv. It'll turn up."

He stared at her.

"Well, I'm sure it will make itself apparent to us in a day or so."

"What are you talking about?"

"Michael, if it's not here, then there are only so many places it can be, and

I will find it."

"Mom, this is key evidence in a homicide investigation. You told me you had it, and now—"

"If yer homicide lads didn't find it in all the time they had, then it can't be that important to them, can it? Besides, there's nothin' I can do in the moment, so sitcheedoon and I'll make ye a cuppa...."

The words just trailed off as Mary-Margaret went into the kitchen. Looking over her shoulder to make sure that Michael had not followed her, she peered out the window of the back door where she could see Arthur walking into the next laneway.

"Is there anythin' else I can get ye, luv?"

"Just a transfer," Michael muttered, wandering over to the chair that Arthur had been sitting in a few minutes earlier and then collapsing into it.

"Ach, luv, it'll all work out in the wash. Have a biscuit while yer waitin' fer yer tea."

"Who was here?"

"Who here where?"

"Here here. I see two teacups. And cookies are still on this plate."

"Ach, that was just me and Arthur havin' a wee chat. He's got a lot on his mind these days, don'tcha know."

Michael stared at the far wall, absently taking a cookie.

"I think you're right, Mom."

"Of course I am, lad. About what?"

"The guy they arrested."

"Indeed. Tell me more."

"I did some digging, and apparently there was another murder where the body was dumped in the ravine. Happened about six months ago."

"So I heard."

"Where?"

"Church, luv. Ye really ought to go. Ye'd be surprised how enlightened ye might become."

"Yeah, well, seems the woman was stabbed multiple times. Looks a lot like Jane Ann's case."

"And they caught…?"

"No."

"So this fella who killed our Jane Ann and the other woman might be one and the same?"

"Possibly."

"And maybe Bobbo didn't kill either of them. We can't have tunnel vision when we are doin' these kinds of investigations, can we?"

Michael stared at his mother, his mouth dropping open.

"Close yer mouth, luv. Flies will get in. Didn't think yer old mam knew anythin' about investigations, did ye? Well, let me tell ye, a woman doesn't raise four children—mostly on her own, God rest yer da's soul— without bein' a bit of a master sleuth."

"I suppose not," Michael said, smiling slightly.

"What evidence do they have on this other murder?"

"I don't know."

"But ye said ye had done some diggin', that the two might be linked?"

"Yes, but—"

"Well then, let's say it's the same fella whose murderin' both of our victims, which would be—"

"They're not *our* victims, Mom."

"Easy to prove if both women were killed by someone who was left-handed."

"I can't."

Mary-Margaret stared at her son.

"Both are ongoing investigations," Michael said.

"And ye are a detective."

"Yes, but not a homicide detective."

"As I'm seein'."

"I can't just go inserting myself into their case."

"Ye already have, haven't ye?"

"I made a couple of phone calls."

"Well, make another one."

"To who, Mom? The pathologist who did the autopsy on the first victim six

169

months ago? 'Hey Doc, I know I have nothing to do with this case, but I was just wondering if the injuries were consistent with a left-handed killer'...?"

"No, luv. But ye have given me an idea. Ach, look at the time. I thought ye said ye were in a hurry?"

"You're not going to call Frank Maloney, are you?"

"And what if I did? Lovely man, is our Francis. In fact, he and I are about due for a date night."

"What you do in your own time is none of my business—"

"No, 'tis not."

"But when you start getting involved in an active police investigation—"

"I shall do no such thing. And if Francis wants to talk about his work with me over dinner, then what am I to do? Poor lad. Not many women would want to go out for a nice steak and kidney pie and hear about how he has to cut—"

"You know what I mean, Mom."

"I do. Now, what is the head man doin' about all of this?"

"Gill? I have no idea. I let him know about the other murder—"

"And did he know about it?"

"I don't know. I assume so. I don't work with him."

"Shall I call our Mandy, then? She'd know."

"Mom, you can't just go calling people—"

"Michael, if ye want to go into Homicide—"

"I don't."

"Or become Police Officer of the Year—"

"Equally unappealing."

"Then ye might want to prick up yer ears. We can't be sittin' by in the comfort of our own home—"

Just as Michael was about to give an answer, Phil ran into the room and hopped up on his lap.

"Get off!" Michael ordered, pushing the dog from his lap.

"There's yer problem, Michael."

"What? That I don't want mud all over my suit? Or throughout my house?"

"No, it runs deeper than that, but here I am, looking like somethin' that would scare off the banshees. I'm off to bed for a nap now. Be sure to let Phil out for a wee piddle before ye go."

She got up and walked toward the stairs.

Chapter Thirty

"And what is this? Having a wee bite before dinner, are we?"

"Gran. You're up." Max said, pausing for a moment before stuffing another entire pastry into his mouth.

"Of course I am. It's not even six p.m. yet."

"I just thought—"

"That I was dead in me bed?"

Seeing the look on Max's face, Mary-Margaret pulled him into a hug, forcing him to hold up his skinny arms to avoid covering her with the icing sugar on his fingers.

"Ach. No worries there, lad. I'll be risin' and shinin' for many days to come. Now, dinner. What's it going to be?"

Releasing Max, she made her way to the refrigerator.

"Not much to choose from this evenin'," she said with a grimace. "What say you we go to O'Leary's? My treat. It's not quite just around the corner from here, but it'll do. Now do whatever it is needs doin' while I find me keys."

Hearing the word keys, Phil woke up from what appeared to be a dead sleep on one of the wingback chairs in the living room and raced into the kitchen, where he danced at her feet.

"And before we get carried away with ourselves, can ye take wee Phil—"

"Already did, Gran."

"Ye cheeky dog," Mary-Margaret said, looking down at the dog, who seemed to smile up at her before strutting back to the living room chair.

"Is your friend ever going to take her dog back?"

"Tirin' ye out, is he?"

"No, I just thought that, well, Dad said—"

"And there's yer problem, me lamb. What yer da has to say has nothin' to do with what ye are thinkin'. Now, are we going to be chewin' the fat, or are we goin' to have ourselves a lovely dinner out?"

"Dinner out."

"Grand. Get yer coat."

* * *

"Mary-Margaret," Frank called out from across the pub.

"Francis," Mary-Margaret replied, looking over at Max so that Frank would know she was not alone.

"If ye had told me ye were comin', I coulda picked ye up."

"And what makes ye think I knew we were comin' here? Wasn't I just looking in the deep freeze not half an hour ago, sayin' as how there was nothin' to eat and decided we might want to come for a good hot dinner here, Max?"

"Yeah."

"And so, Francis, there was absolutely no forethought put into it. Wouldn't ye agree, Max? And while ye are at it, luv, can ye find us a table."

"For three?" Frank said as he walked towards her, a twinkle in his eye.

"For three," Mary-Margaret agreed, "over in the corner somewhere?"

"Sure, Gran."

"I must say, it is a treat to see you, Mary-Margaret," Frank said as Max made his way to the other side of the small pub.

"Before we sit down with the lad, I've a couple of questions to ask of ye."

"Nothing too personal, I hope?"

"Behave yerself, Francis. There's a child present," she replied with a wink. "Ye are sure whoever it was who killed Jane Ann was left-handed?"

"Sure."

"Do ye know anythin' about another murder?"

"I know about a lot of murders, Mary-Margaret. If ye are hopin' fer me to answer before we sit with the lad, ye might want to be a bit more specific."

"A woman. Maybe like Jane Ann."

"Dead?"

"Now, who's wastin' words?"

"Me job is to slice and dice 'em, luv. I don't get involved in the hereafter, either where God or the police are concerned."

"Has there been another woman's body brought in with stab wounds like Jane Ann's done by a left-handed fella? Maybe about six months ago?"

"There's been dozens on my table since then, Mary-Margaret. I don't think I could even begin to remember even if I wanted to."

"Brought in from the ravine as Jane Ann?"

"I don't notice where they come from, luv. I just pull 'em out of the cooler."

"Stab wounds?"

"Luv, I don't know."

"Ye have about five seconds to think."

Mary-Margaret waved over to Max, who had secured a table and was now texting on his cell.

"Give me ten while I grab me pint o' the bar," Frank said with a sigh, reaching over to pick up his glass and saying something to the bartender.

Mary-Margaret smiled again toward Max, who, looking up from his phone, waved to her with both arms.

"I see ye, luv. Just standin' by for Francis," she called to him. "Give us a moment, will ye?"

Max's attention returned to the screen.

"Come to think of it," Frank said, taking a sip of his beer as he turned back to Mary-Margaret, "I do recall one particularly brutal—"

"That would likely be it. Talk fast." Mary-Margaret glanced over at Max, who was fully absorbed in his phone again.

"Not that old, she was. Likely a pretty girl, too. Face was just slashed to bits."

"Left-handed?"

"Indeed. Thought it was a domestic—those get so violent. She was found in a ravine."

"Which ravine?"

"I don't know, luv. A ravine with a lot o' trees in it."

"And how would ye know this?"

"Scrapes and scratches and such on the body. Consistent-like with bein' dragged through the woods. And clay. There was clay as well."

"Where?"

"Was all caked in her hair. All of it. She was naked."

"We'll discuss this later," Mary-Margaret said with a deep breath as they took the dozen or so steps to the table Max had chosen. "Now, are ye here with us or lost to yer screen time, Max?"

"I was just waiting for you guys."

"And here we are. Francis, did ye happen to order me a half-pint of—"

"Indeed, I did." He smiled as the young server set the glass down beside her.

"And what will ye be havin', Max?"

"The chicken fingers look good."

"Perhaps for ye, Max, but I think I'll have the steak-and-kidney. Francis, what'll it be for ye? My treat."

"'Tis very kind of ye, Mary-Margaret, but I've already eaten." He saw her look of disappointment. "Doesn't mean I can't finish me pint with ye. And then I'm off. Me day starts early, and mine is not the kind o' job ye can be sleepin' at."

"Suit yerself then. Chicken fingers for the lad, steak-and-kidney for me, and a plate of chips to share," Mary-Margaret told the server, passing her the menus.

"So are ye goin' be a policeman like yer da, then, Max?"

"No," Max answered, checking his phone one last time before shoving it in his pocket.

Mary-Margaret raised her glass. "Sláinte."

"Sláinte," Frank replied, raising his.

"It's not that I don't think it's a good job or anything like that," Max said. "It's just not something I'd like to do."

"Ah. Very good." Frank nodded awkwardly. "'Tis the blood and guts that

175

gets ye, is it?"

"Francis. We'll be having our meal in front of us shortly," Mary-Margaret scolded.

"I'm askin' me man, not ye, and there be no food now, is there?" Frank said grandly, looking pleased at having made some connection with Mary-Margaret's grandson.

"No, I don't think that would bother me," Max said. "Hey, you're the morgue guy, aren't you?"

"Supposin' I am? "

"You must see lots of neat stuff."

"Suppose I do? "

"Like what?"

"Dunno. We do an autopsy every hour or so…"

"Is it true," Max asked, leaning towards Frank, "that your hair keeps growing even after you're dead? Or your fingernails? I heard—"

"No. Nothin' grows after ye are dead, lad."

"Do you ever figure out who the killer is before the D's do?"

"The wha'?" Frank said with a smile.

"D's. You know. Detectives. Cops."

"A right clever lad is yer grandson, Mary-Margaret. Ye mean like yer da? Sometimes. Well, no. That's a lie. We sometimes figure it out alongside 'em."

"How?"

"Well, like I was just tellin' yer gran here, we had a case just a couple of days back wherein the body had clay in the scalp hair—"

"Francis, not that I think this is appropriate language at a table in a public house, nor do I believe we should continue this discussion, but didn't the one ye were just tellin' me about five minutes ago also have clay in her hair?"

"So she did, me luv. Both had clay in their hair."

"This is so cool," Max said, his eyes as wide as saucers.

"Mind," Mary-Margaret said with a nod.

"Right," Frank nodded back.

"Oh, come on. I do watch TV, you know!" Max said, smiling smugly.

Mary-Margaret arched her eyebrows and was silent for a moment before continuing.

"And scratch marks like the other one?"

"I believe so," replied Frank.

"From the trees in the ravine?"

"Indeed."

"Left-handed. Ravine."

"Yeah. 'Tis so."

"Are ye thinkin' at all what I'm thinkin', Francis?"

"That 'tis the same fella? Could be."

"Chicken fingers?" the server asked, placing the plate in front of Max at his nod but hesitating before setting the other plate down.

"That'll be mine, luv. Me man here is not eatin'. Says he already did. Ye did, did ye not? Eat, I mean, Francis? I can't have ye walking' away from the table hungry."

"Indeed, I have. Ye here can attest to it, can't ye?"

"Yes, he did. Would you like to keep your bill at the bar, sir, or do you want it transferred?"

"Onto my bill, thank ye," Mary-Margaret directed.

"No. I can't have the lady payin'—"

"'Tis done, Francis. Now, Max, ye must have been hungry. And put yer eyes back in yer head, luv. No need to tell yer da about any of this, yeah?"

Chapter Thirty-One

While she could hardly say that there ever was a time when Father Miguel was at his best, Mary-Margaret had to admit that he did a very good funeral Mass. Jane Ann Hill's was no exception.

"Arthur, luv, I'm pleased that ye have attended, but I'm a bit confused by yer getup," she said to her friend, choosing her words carefully as the two got into her car to join the procession to the cemetery. "Tell me ye aren't still takin' pictures by bashin' yer head."

"Blending in, MM," Arthur said, adjusting the netting on the black pillbox hat that he had wedged down on a gray wig that managed to fit even worse than the one he had worn at the candlelight vigil. "And no pictures. This is a funeral."

"Fair enough," she said with a nod, then noticing the white tennis shoes under the long black dress Arthur was wearing, added, "Goin' forward, however, bear in mind, luv, that if ye are goin' to try to be…old, ye can't be wearin' sport shoes to somethin' like this. I don't mean that as a criticism, luv."

"Not at all, MM. I was running a bit low on my Old-Lady-Funeral outfits. And after the other night, there was no way I was going to wear anything like those horrible lace-ups again. My feet just couldn't take it."

"Right. Well, I suppose no one was truly lookin' at ye anyway. So what did ye think of the funeral, now?" she asked, switching on her four-way blinkers as she put the car in gear and fell into place in the procession to the cemetery.

"Full house."

"Indeed. Lovely, wasn't it?"

"Including all of the cops on the case, speaking of not blending in."

"Ach, I know. They try, don't they? Speakin' of which, should they not have had a paid escort on this one? As if getting out of the parking lot wasn't a challenge enough, I've got miserable sods like this tryin' to cut across the roadway in front of me. Oi!" she yelled as she rolled down her window and then poked her head out, "'Tis a funeral, this is. D'ye not see me flashin' lights or the sign on me bonnet?"

"He's just trying to get across the intersection, MM. It's a four-way, and he's been waiting a while."

"And he can wait a while longer." Mary-Margaret accelerated to diminish the gap between her car and the one in front, then slammed on the brakes to avoid rear-ending it.

"There is no regard for the dead, Arthur. None."

"Yes, well," Arthur said somewhat shakily, withdrawing the hand he had flung out onto the dashboard in anticipation of a crash.

"But ye were sayin'?"

"Right. So the cops were there at the back. Place was packed with what I'm assuming were people from the co-op."

"Was lovely, wasn't it? To be that well-regarded to have the entire place turn out. Lovely."

"And I noticed a guy I'm assuming was her boyfriend?"

"What makes ye say that, luv?"

"Did you see the way he was looking around at everyone? If looks could kill, we'd have back-to-back funerals going on. God, I wish I had got the XXL pantyhose. I can hardly feel my feet, even with these shoes." He groaned.

"Welcome to me world, luv."

They drove on for several minutes as the funeral procession snaked its way through the city, with the cars speeding up to get through traffic lights before they turned red or if they got caught on the other side once the lights turned green again. Remarkably, the entire procession arrived intact at its destination. Despite having started somewhere in the middle, Mary-Margaret's Dauphine had somehow ended up closer to the end.

"It's just come to me now: how shall I introduce ye, should anyone ask?"

"Just tell people that I'm your sister from over 'ome."

"I see," Mary-Margaret said, pulling into the cemetery. "And what name shall I provide?"

"Bernadette," Arthur said after a moment's thought.

"Bernadette, it is." She grabbed her purse from the back seat before climbing out and heading towards the open grave.

"I'm just going to hang back, if you don't mind, MM," Arthur said. "I can get a better sense of the mourners here and maybe gather a bit more intel. Bet you didn't even notice I have a camera in the brooch on my dress, did you?"

"I thought you said—"

"No pictures at the funeral? I did. This is the graveside."

"Ach. Just try to keep the wailing to a minimum this time, please?"

* * *

"The least he could do—and I've mentioned it to Umberto many times before—is put down more sod or whatever it is they put down to cover the mud bath they make of the gravesite. This is not the first time I've nearly sunk knee-deep into it at an interment here. Look at them, Arthur." Mary-Margaret gestured indignantly at her muddied shoes when she reached her car where Arthur had been standing. "Ruined."

"I'd hardly say ruined, MM."

"Well, I would. Look at this." She stopped in front of Arthur and pointed to the inch and a half of mud caked on her shoe. "Ye can't get that off with a wet cloth now, can ye?"

"Leave them with me when we get back, and I'll clean them off at my place. I've got something that will make them as good as new."

"Ye are a godsend, Arth—I mean, Bernadette."

"I've got a shammy in my purse. I'll give them a wipe before you get in the car."

"Not that I'm ungrateful, luv, but why would ye have such a thing?"

"As a trained undercover agent, I never know what to expect, MM. While this is hardly the raison d'être, one never knows when one might have to wipe something down in my business."

"And what would yer business be at the moment?"

"MM, you surprise me," Arthur said, kneeling down in his tent-like dress to wipe off her shoes. "I am so not just a cleaner, or a techno-wizard, or a master—or mistress—of disguises. I am a trained and licensed private investigator, which I don't think you knew, and I am going to use all of my training and experience to help you find your friend's killer. In fact, I've got enough photos of everyone here to fill a book."

"Grand, luv. That's grand. Ach, look at those maniacs tearin' away. 'Tis a funeral luncheon we're off to, not a race at Mondello Park! Get in, luv. By the way, this lot is pressin' out. I wouldn't be surprised if there were no sandwiches left at O'Leary's if we don't fire up the coal."

Arthur hopped in the car as Mary-Margaret dropped the transmission into drive and squealed away from the gravesite.

"And why didn't ye tell me ye were a licensed PI earlier?"

"I just got my license in the mail this morning."

"From one of those click-and-mail places on the internet?"

"Something like that."

All was quiet for a few moments as she waited for a few more cars to leave before maneuvering her way to the cemetery entrance.

"Oh," Arthur suddenly said, "I've also got the blood types and a match off that glove you gave me."

Mary-Margaret looked over at him with such focus that she had to slam on the brakes to avoid crashing into a leaning tombstone that was suddenly in front of them. "Jesus, Mary, and Joseph," she gasped. "Since when did they put roundabouts in cemeteries?"

"We came through this way," Arthur said, once again releasing the dashboard from his hand.

"So how did you manage to get blood types and a…did ye say a match?"

"Well, not a match per se. More like a type."

"So why did ye say a match?"

"Sounded sexier."

"Arth—Bern—Arthur, if there's one thing ye need to know if we are goin' to be doin' this together: I don't want sexy."

"I don't believe that, MM. In fact, I bet you were quite something back in the day."

"Back in the day? I still am quite somethin'! Just ask—"

"Who?"

"Never ye mind. Now, what can ye tell me about this glove of ours?"

"Two blood types on the glove. Not surprising. One was probably the deceased's, and the other would be the murderer's. One was O Negative, the other was A Positive."

"And ye would know this how?"

"I did a blood analysis," Arthur replied matter-of-factly.

"How did ye manage that?"

"Oh, I ordered this kit online. And then all I had to do was—"

"Is there nothin' ye can't get online?" Mary-Margaret said. "But one thing, and I should have noticed at the time but did not: Was the glove ye took a right or left one?"

"Right."

"So it could have belonged to Jane Ann's murderer."

"Why do you say that?"

"Ach, ye are soundin' more like me Michael every moment, Arthur." She slipped into a parking spot on the street close to the pub. "The logic behind it is too compli—"

"Well, if we're going to be in this together, you need to know that I can follow anyone's logic better than—"

"So be it. Consider, then, that ye are draggin' someone. Maybe they're still alive, although I don't think Jane Ann was. Likely, ye are just afraid they are. If ye had but one hand to drag them with, which hand would it be?"

"My right hand."

"Really? Then maybe I'm wrong. If it was me, I'd be usin' me left. Leave me right hand free to do whatever needs doin'."

"I'm left-handed."

"So ye can attest to what I am about to say: The right hand would be pulling the body, the left hand—the gloved hand—would be free in case ye needed to give yer victim another stab."

"Brilliant, MM."

"Indeed, Arth—Bernadette. Prepare yerself to be doin' a wee bit of investigation at this reception," she said as she pulled the car over to the curb and pulled the parking brake up.

"We're not the only ones," Arthur said, pointing to the two homicide detectives just getting out of the sedan parked in front of them.

"Mrs. O'Shea," Detective Gill said, waiting on the sidewalk by the unmarked police car for Mary-Margaret and Arthur to walk past them. "Sorry for your loss."

"Wish I could be sayin' the same to ye, but I suppose without me loss, ye wouldn't have a job, would ye?"

"What do you mean?"

"It was a joke, lad. Ye are homicide investigators. Without a homicide, ye have nothin'. Ach, I miss our Mandy. Great lot of craic, that one."

"We were just wondering if we could talk to your..." Gill paused as he looked Arthur up and down, "...friend here, for a moment."

"Me friend? She's not me friend. This is me sister, Bernadette, from over 'ome." Mary-Margaret took Arthur's arm, smiling warmly at him.

"Bernadette, is it?" Gill repeated, stretching out his hand.

"Indeed. Me sister, Bernadette. Came over just the other night, didn't ye, luv?"

"Yes. That's right. Flew in just the other night, did I," Arthur replied with an attempt at a heavy brogue, not taking his hand.

"What flight?" Gill asked, bringing his hand back to his side.

"Ummm..."

"The flight that came over from Ireland, lad. Ach, ye and me Michael, ye call yerselves investigators, and yet ye miss the obvious. Come on, luv. Let's take ourselves inside." She gave Arthur a gentle nudge in the small of his back.

"Just a minute, Mrs. O'Shea. We noticed that your...sister was taking pictures at the gravesite, and we'd like to have a look at what she has."

MARY-MARGARET AND THE CASE OF THE LAPSED PARISHIONER

"Ye are jokin' now, are ye? Here's me sister, comin' over to our fair land to see how we do things here, and ye are wantin' to confiscate her photos? Where is the justice, lad? And the decency? We've barely left the grave of me dear friend, and ye are conductin' an inquisition right here, right now, on the sidewalk in front of the pub. With not even the decency to wait until we've paid our final respects with a toast."

"It's just, uh, Bernadette seems a bit...out of place—"

"Well, of course, she's out of place. She has just been steppin' off the plane not but a few hours—"

"I thought you said she came a couple of days ago."

"A couple of days, a few hours... It's all the same when ye are in the state I've been in. Have a wee bit of mercy, lads."

The two detectives looked Arthur up and down again, as did Mary-Margaret.

"Ach, it's the clothin', isn't it? Well, as ye can imagine, dear Bernadette never intended to go to a funeral on her visit to her sister, did ye, luv? And when she saw what a state I was in today, she was adamant that I not go alone, weren't ye, luv? And if we were home, she'd have driven me, but with the cars on the wrong side of the road over here—isn't that what ye say back home, luv?—it was all just too confusin' for her, so she's just tagged along with me. But not a stitch of clothin' suitable for a funeral, so we just threw somethin' together, didn't we, luv? Last minute-like."

"Yes. That's exactly what we did."

"Do you have any identification, ma'am?" Gill said.

"Has she done anythin' wrong? Me stars! Here she is, a guest in this free country, comin' all the way from Ireland, and ye are given' her the Fifth.

"Mary-Margaret," Chrystal Hill called out from the front door of the pub. "We're starting to say a few words, and I'd really like you to be here for it."

"Me and me sister, Bernadette, will be right there, luv," Mary-Margaret called back. "Excuse me, gentlemen, but the orphan of the deceased is callin' for us."

With that, she pushed her way past the two homicide investigators, holding Arthur's arm lightly as she pulled him along with her.

"We will be having a word with you, Bernadette," Detective Gill called after the two.

"Perhaps yer time would be better spent findin' the killer than waitin' outside of a pub for a couple of ladies to finish a half-pint at a funeral reception," Mary-Margaret shouted back.

"You are fierce," Arthur said, eyes glowing with admiration.

"Oh, ye have not heard the half of it. Wait until I tell me Michael about this. Badges will be turned in before I am done."

Chapter Thirty-Two

"Michael. Ye gave me a start, lad! What are ye doin' here? I thought ye were at work," Mary-Margaret said as she let herself and Arthur into the kitchen through the back door.

"I am," Michael said, his eyes narrowing as he looked at Arthur dressed as he was.

"Do the lot of ye share a brain at that police service of yours? Ye are clearly not—"

"What are the two of you up to?" Michael demanded.

"Now, Michael, is that any tone to be usin' with yer mam?"

"Only if my mother is messing up an active homicide investigation."

"Which I am not. Now, Bernadette—I mean Arthur, would ye put the kettle on so as we can all have a cuppa?"

"I think I should be going," Arthur replied.

"I think you should be staying," Michael corrected.

"And I think we should all have a cuppa and cool our jets," Mary-Margaret said, filling up the kettle and putting it on the back burner of the stove before going into the dining room. "Now, if ye'll mind yer manners, Michael, we'll all have a seat at the table here and get ourselves sorted."

"Detective Gill called me to tell me to talk to you. Again."

"About what?"

"About taking pictures at a funeral."

"The gravesite."

"Same thing."

"No, it's not. Regardless, the crime bein'…?"

"I think I should go," Arthur said again.

"Absolutely not," Mary-Margaret said. "Arthur and I were at the funeral, 'tis true. And yes, we did take a few snaps. And yes, we do have the glove—"

"The glove? You took the glove?" Michael said, his eyes widening.

"I think I'm late for my next appointment," Arthur said, getting up.

"Sit," both Mary-Margaret and Michael told Arthur.

"I thought ye knew that we had the glove," Mary-Margaert said to Michael.

"Mom, you are now tampering with evidence."

"Yer lads missed it, and I did not. What blood type is the lad ye have in yer cells?"

"He's not in custody anymore. He's been released on conditions. And how should I know?"

"Ach. And ye wonder why I've involved meself. Michael, we found two blood types on the glove. One is O Negative, and that would be Jane Ann's—"

"How do you know this?" Michael said, leaning back in his chair.

"I asked Chrystal. Or as I believe ye might say in your world, I did some investigatin'. The other is A Positive."

Michael took a deep breath and a slow sip of his tea.

"And what do we know of the other murder, since ye were likely sendin' Bobbo upstairs for both."

Michael paused a moment, then looked over at Arthur and back to his mother.

"She was also a resident of the co-op. Single. Middle-aged. No known family. No known enemies. Worked as a telemarketer—"

"I thought ye said she had no known enemies," Mary-Margaret interrupted, a sparkle in her eyes.

"You are The Bomb," Arthur said with a laugh.

"Oh, and before I forget, Michael, should anyone ask, yer auntie is over from Ireland for a wee visit."

"I don't even want to know," Michael said, letting out a long sigh. "Anyway, it would appear that she was murdered in her apartment—"

"Just like Jane Ann," Mary-Margaret said, her back straightening.

"And her body was found in the ravine."

"And no one thought to link the two?"

"No, Mom," Michael said, looking directly at his mother. "No one thought to tell you that they'd linked the two."

Mary-Margaret looked uncomprehendingly at her son before continuing.

"Now, Michael, we have snaps of everyone who was at the interment and the reception. While Arthur—oh, yer aunties name is Bernadette, should anyone ask—isn't certain—"

"Pretty certain," Arthur cut in.

"Certain enough that the fella next door wasn't there."

"And why would he be?"

"Common courtesy," Mary-Margaret stated. "And they were friendly, the two of them were."

"Friendly like a nod in the hallway, or friendly like sharing a bed?"

"Michael," Mary-Margaret gasped.

"Well?" he said, dunking his cookie in his tea.

"Friendly as in a nod in the hallway or maybe a cuppa tea together sort of way, from what Chrystal was tellin' me, although they may have had a fallin' out of sorts that put Jane Ann off of him."

"Did you tell this to Detective Gill?"

"He never asked."

Michael shook his head.

"Regardless, a man goes to his neighbor's funeral where I come from. No excuse. She was his direct neighbor. A friend, even. Who would miss that? Speakin' of which, did ye see Jane Ann's lad, Arthur?"

"No, I didn't," Arthur said.

"That say's somethin' right there, doesn't it? Although," Mary-Margaret reconsidered, "it might be hard for him to get around without his car. What say ye, Michael?"

"About what?"

"The car. Why do yer lads still have Jerry's car?"

"They are investigating him for something else," Michael said after a short pause.

"Like what?" Mary-Margaret asked.

"Like I don't know."

"Michael…." Mary-Margaret looked directly at her son, her right eyebrow raised practically into her hairline.

"Resistance is futile," Arthur murmured.

Michael paused again..

"There have been a number of thefts from the factory where Jerry—"

"He's a cookie thief? I knew he was into somethin'. He had those shifty little eyes. How was he doin' it, lad? Takin' a box at a time? Sellin' them on the black market? It was like that back home, after the war. A lass would kill her best cousin for a few feet of lace back then. I knew it."

"Hardly, Mom."

Mary-Margaret and Arthur both sat on the edges of their chairs. Michael said nothing.

"Ach!" Mary-Margaret exclaimed, throwing her hands up. "Ye can't leave us hangin'."

"I've already said too much."

"And who would I be tellin'? Or are ye imaginin' me callin' up Janelle Austin with me hot tip. 'Janelle, luv, 'tis yer old pal Mary-Margaret. I've got a story about a lad who could have been a murderer but settled for bein' a cookie thief. If ye get yer self and yer fancy boots down here right now, I'll give ye an exclusive.' I'm seein' it, Michael. As a matter of fact, ye had better boil another kettle, Arthur. She'll be at the door before Michael finishes fillin' us in."

"Mom, come on," Michael said.

"Don't come on me, Michael. Tell us the lot of it."

Michael leaned back in his chair and sighed.

"And don't ye be sighin' again unless ye are gaspin' for air. Now," Mary-Margaret said, tapping her index finger on the table. "Out with it."

"Jerry LaMarshe wasn't stealing a box or two of cookies. He was stealing trailer loads full. He was brought in to speak to Homicide because he was Jane Ann's boyfriend. That's the usual thing. Unbeknownst to Gill, he was also under surveillance by Major Crime."

"This sounds so sexy," Arthur said.

"Stealin' cookies is not sexy, Arthur," Mary-Margaret said. "I'm seein' all of the faces of those wee smallies, sittin' at the table expectin' their tea and not a cookie to be found. Would have been better if he had murdered Jane Ann, if ye asked me."

"Sure," Michael said, rubbing his forehead.

"Wait a minute," Arthur said. "You mean to say this guy would walk up to some random and say, 'Hey buddy, want to buy some truckloads of cookies?' And then drop them off?"

Michael set his head down into his hands and rubbed it before looking over at Arthur.

"No. LaMarshe was in financial trouble. And he had some friends who owned a couple of grocery store franchises. So he approached his buddies, telling them that he could get them truckloads of cookies to sell at their franchises for a highly discounted price."

"So if Jerry didn't use his car to take the cookies, what are yer lads looking for?"

"He allegedly also sold a quantity of drugs to these guys."

"So this is really about drugs, not cookies," Mary-Margaret said.

"Mostly, although they don't believe he set out to sell drugs. The running theory is that LaMarshe had a bigger financial problem than selling trailer loads of stolen cookies could solve, so he had to get creative. He asked his franchise-owning buddies if there was anything else he could do to make money, and they suggested running drugs."

"So why not run them in the trailers?" Mary-Margaret asked.

"Whoa," Arthur said. "That would be a *huge* amount of drugs."

"Exactly. They just needed a guy to do some deliveries to their dealers on the street."

"So he's a drug-dealin' cookie thief, but not a murderer is what ye're tellin' me."

"Pretty much."

"Well," Mary-Margaret said. "That's somethin', then."

All three of them sat in silence for a few minutes.

"Arthur, did ye get that kettle boilin'?"

190

"No, why? Is Janelle Austin coming over?"

"Ye've missed yer callin', lad. Ring up Graham Norton and let him know he's off the show. I'm seein' that our cups...."

Arthur was in the kitchen with the water filling the kettle before Mary-Margaret could finish.

"Michael, that only leaves us with one suspect."

"Really?"

"It has to be the neighbor."

"A man misses a funeral. That doesn't make him a killer," Michael said.

"Unless he lives in the apartment that the first murdered woman lived in," Mary-Margaret said with a confident nod.

"And does he?" Arthur asked, returning to the table.

"He might."

Both Arthur and Michael looked at Mary-Margaret.

"How else did he get in without bein' voted in? 'Tis as plain as the brain in Laura-Jean McQueen's head. He got in because his girlfriend was murdered. And how do I know this, ye ask?"

"I have no clue," said Michael.

"Nancy, the super, told me that the neighbor was datin' someone in the co-op, but she died. Her body was found in the ravine. I assumed the poor soul had ended her own life, but now I'm wonderin'. Next thing ye know, our man is livin' in a highy sought-after co-op. And how do ye think he jumped the queue?"

"Maybe a lot of units came up at once," Michael said.

"'Tis unlikely in a place like that. And then there's the matter of the ravine. How many bodies do ye find in that place?"

"I have no idea, Mom."

"Ye do, Michael," she said, her voice raising. "The girlfriend found in the ravine and the woman found murdered in the ravine six months ago are one and the same."

"Whoa," said Arthur.

"We don't know that for sure," Michael replied calmly.

Only the tapping of wee Phil's toenails on the hardwood floor could be heard as everyone sat in silence.

"Ye know somethin' more, don't ye?" Mary-Margaret said, looking closely at her son.

Arthur pulled his chair in closer.

"No, I—"

"Michael, how long have I been yer mam and known every breath ye take?"

"Mom, this is—"

"I think ye are just now seein' that it's the neighbor."

"I want you and Arthur to give me all of the photos you took today," Michael said, quickly getting up from his seat. "I want you to give me the glove. And I want—"

"I'll make ye a deal, Michael," Mary-Margaret said, looking up at her son. "Give us twenty-four hours and, if we haven't found the murderer, we'll turn over everythin', won't we, Arthur?"

"Twenty-four hours," Arthur said, nodding his head in agreement..

"I'm not making any deals," Michael said firmly, stepping back from the table to address them both. "If you won't give me what I'm asking for, I'll arrest both of you for obstruct and then get a warrant and seize the glove and the photos ."

Twenty-four hours, luv, or it's all yours. Eazy Peazy."

"Eazy Peazy," Arthur echoed.

"What am I going to tell Gill?"

"Now tell yer man Gill that yer mam has no photos. Don't breathe a word about the glove. Ye are goin' to find it yerself in twenty-four hours' time if Arthur and I haven't solved the murder."

Chapter Thirty-Three

"**E**xcuse me," Arthur said, whacking the ground with a white cane, "but I'm here to visit my friend at the co-op and can't seem to find the front door."

Mary-Margaret looked through the passenger window at the spectacle on the sidewalk beside her parked car and smiled. With his Gilligan hat, Jackie O sunglasses, long trench coat, and white cane that was likely a hockey stick in its previous life, Arthur was quite a sight to behold. She got out of her car and approached him.

"It's me, Arthur," he whispered loudly, pulling down the dark glasses that hid his eyes.

"I know it's ye, Arthur," Mary-Margaret said.

"Impossible. This is my best disguise ever."

"Just don't hit the side of me car with yer stick," Mary-Margaret said.

"No worries, MM. I just can't come out of character. These walls," Arthur said, waving towards the co-op, "have eyes. Never know who's watching. Never too early to get into character."

He squinted in the morning sunlight and pushed his glasses back onto his face.

"And why this particular get up, might I ask?" Mary-Margaret said.

"Because no one is going to think that a blind guy is looking for a murderer."

"That's fair."

"Here's the plan: You do the door knock. I'll stand back. I've got a video camera built into the side of these glasses, so while you're talking to the perp, I'll be in the hallway behind you, taking quick pictures of the inside of his apartment."

"Grand. Now, I didn't think of this before this moment, but what if he's not home?"

"Even better," Arthur said with a smile, opening his trench coat to show a display of screwdrivers and hacksaws sewn into the left panel.

"Do you know how to use any of those tools, luv?"

"Not really, but it can't be that hard."

Feeling less than confident, Mary-Margaret looked over at the co-op and saw a young man coming out.

"Can ye hold the door for us then, lad?" Mary-Margaret hollered out.

Mary-Margaret walked briskly towards the entrance of the co-op.

Tap, tap, tap. Tap tap tap tap came the sound of Arthur's white cane.

"Catch up, lad," Mary-Margaret said to Arthur.

"I can't. I'm blind. You go," Arthur said, wandering back and forth on the sidewalk in front of the building.

"Excuse me," Mary-Margaret called out to the young man.

"We're not supposed to—"

"Ta, luv. I'm no stranger here," Mary-Margaret said as she took hold of the door with enough force to pull it away from the young man. "I'm visitin' Mr. Fisher."

She smiled warmly at him as he gingerly stepped out onto the sidewalk.

Thwack! Arthur's stick hit the man's shin straight on.

"Oh, excuse me, sir or madam."

"Oh, no. No. Entirely my fault," the young man said, rubbing his shin. "Is there something you're looking—uh, I mean..."

"No, just out for a stroll," Arthur replied, crisscrossing the sidewalk as he walked away from the man.

The man gave Arthur one last look before hurrying across the street to a waiting car.

"You see," Arthur said, zigzagging towards the front door of the building as the car drove off. "Eyes everywhere. Let me take your arm, MM. I wouldn't be surprised if someone is watching us right now from that camera."

"Indeed," Mary-Margaret said, noting the security camera in the lobby as she led Arthur into the hallway. "Hrmph," she huffed, noticing the nameplate on her friend's door gone. "Doesn't take long before they forget, does it? Barely in the ground, is she, and—"

"Shh. Someone's coming," Arthur said.

A wiry man, no taller than Mary-Margaret but looking to be half her weight, was behind them. It was Mr. Fisher.

Mary-Margaret stood looking around the hallway as if she was in an art gallery, looking at the masterpieces hung on the wall. Arthur released himself from her and turned and walked very slowly towards the man, thrashing his hockey stick/cane from side to side, smashing the walls as he went.

"Do you need help?" Mr. Fisher asked as he approached the door beside Jane Ann's.

"Just went blind," Arthur said, looking above the man's head. "Which is not exactly true. I have been blind for most of my life, but my guide dog, Thadeus, just..." He began to wail.

"What me friend is tryin' to say," Mary-Margaret jumped in, rubbing Arthur's back as she approached him, "was that he's in a bit of a state on account of the dog, ye see, and, well, we were wonderin' if ye might have a glass of water ye could give the lad."

Mr. Fisher looked Mary-Margaret up and down, and then looked Arthur over.

"He's diabetic as well," she added.

The man put his key in the lock and opened the door.

Mary-Margaret looked expectantly at Mr. Fisher. "Likely to pass out is where I'm goin' with this."

"Yeah. Sure. C'mon in. Place is a bit of a mess."

"I'm blind. I won't notice," Arthur said as he followed Mary-Margaret inside the apartment.

"Ta, luv. Ach, ye are a saint." She reached in front of Arthur to take the glass of water from Mr. Fisher. "While he may look steady, ye must recall that me friend here is blind and is just takin' a stab at knowin' what ye are handin' and where. Isn't that so...Ar—Calvin?"

"True that, MM. I mean, MJ. Blind as a bat. Not many visually impaired people are, you know. In fact—"

"Why don't ye just drink yer water, luv, and we can leave our new friend to himself," Mary-Margaret said, cutting off what she feared would be one of Arthur's overly involved explanations. "Would ye mind puttin' a spoonful of sugar in it? Calvin, here, is diabetic. A glass of water isn't likely to do much for him as it is."

Their reluctant host opened a cupboard and retrieved a bag of sugar, pouring some into the glass Arthur was holding.

Mary-Margaret glanced around the room.

"Catholic, are ye?" she said.

"No. Why do you ask?" Mr. Fisher responded.

"Just the ladies' chain with a crucifix there on the air con." Mary-Margaret pointed to a silver necklace with a small crucifix sitting on top of the window air conditioner.

"Oh, that. It's just something a friend of mine left."

"Really? Seems a bit odd, no? Leavin' a necklace, much less one with a crucifix and all, lyin' about, unless she stayed the night and left in a hurry?"

Forgetting himself, Arthur pulled up his sunglasses and shot a deadly glance at Mary-Margaret.

"I'm just sayin'. A good-lookin' single lad like ye likely has quite a few callers of the female persuasion. Am I right, or am I right?"

"That's really none of your business. Your friend has had his glass of sugar water. Would you mind leaving now, please? And haven't I seen you before?"

"Ye know," Mary-Margaret continued, "Now that me eyes are fixed on it, I believe I've seen that crucifix before."

"Really? They all look the same to me," the man said with an uneasy laugh.

"I wouldn't know. I'm blind," Arthur said, moving his head awkwardly as he positioned the lens of the video camera on his glasses into place.

"You okay, bud?" Mr. Fisher asked, looking more closely at Arthur.

"It's an inner ear thing. When I get dehydrated—"

"I thought you were a diabetic." Mr. Fisher looked closely at Arthur.

"Ach, did I say he was diabetic? I meant dehydrated," Mary-Margaret cut in. "Good thing I didn't say dead."

"Mary-Margaret," Arthur said with a gasp.

"I thought your name was MJ?" Mr. Fisher said, looking over at Mary-Margaret.

"It's the dehydration. And now, likely, the sugar blast. Sends the lad off his pins, mentally speakin'," she explained, backing towards the door.

"Maybe your friend should sit down for a moment," Mr. Fisher suggested, pointing towards the couch while Arthur continued to twitch, the camera in his glasses rolling. "You might also want to take a seat."

"No, there's no need for tha—"

"You might as well all sit down for a few moments. And then I've got to get back to my work."

"Which is what, Mister…?"

"Fisher. Mister Fisher."

"And ye have no first name?"

"Not that you need to be aware of," Mr. Fisher replied.

Chapter Thirty-Four

"Well, this is cozy, isn't it?" Mary-Margaret said, noting that this apartment was a mirror of Jane Ann's.

"I'm sorry I have nothing but water to offer you," Mr. Fisher said, motioning for his guests to sit down on the couch. "Unless you want some sugar in it as well."

"Not to worry, lad. And since we are all gettin' on so well—" Mary-Margaret said, making room for Arthur to sit beside her.

"Who said we were getting on well?" Mr. Fisher said.

"Me name is Mary-Margaret O'Shea," she continued. "Me blind friend, Calvin, whose real name is Arthur, only calls me MJ as a bit of an inside joke, don't ye, lad? It's a long story, the logic behind it is too complicated for me to explain now, considerin' that we've already taken up so much of yer time, which is to say, thank ye for your hospitality, but we—"

"No, please," Mr. Fisher said with a smile. "Stay."

"About that necklace with the crucifix on it, then," Mary-Margaret said while Arthur continued to scan the room.

"You seem particularly interested in it. Why?"

"Ye see, I'm…I was…the secretary over at St. Francis of Assisi, and every year, we award crucifixes that look exactly like the one ye have right there—"

"Who knew? My neighbor, the one who used to live next door, gave it to me. I guess she got some award from your church once upon a time," Mr. Fisher said abruptly.

Arthur stopped scanning the room and looked quickly over at Mary-Margaret.

"She used to wear it around her neck, and when I last saw her I commented on it, and she insisted that I take it. And that's where I guess I left it. Satisfied?"

"I find that hard to believe," Mary-Margaret said, pushing her chin out.

Mr. Fisher smiled. "She and I were quite close towards the end."

"Really?" Mary-Margaret raised an eyebrow. "I heard differently. And, if ye were so close, why weren't ye at her—"

Arthur jabbed her in the ribs with his elbow.

"Funeral? That's what you were going to say, wasn't it? I was busy. Not that it's any of your business. But, just to be clear, I've already spoken to the police. I had nothing to do with my neighbor's death."

"I'm not so sure." Arthur lowered his glasses to look up at Mr. Fisher.

"For a blind man, you have very clear eyes," Mr. Fisher said with a smile.

"Yes, I do. It's a very rare type of—"

"Oh, cut the crap," Mr. Fisher said calmly. "You and Miss Marple here are trying to solve a murder mystery. Don't think I haven't noticed her snooping around with her cop buddies. Now, I've let you inside my place to have a look around, I've given this guy something to drink, I've told you why I have that crucifix, and now I think we can all just carry on our merry way, don't you?"

"What blood type are you, Mr. Fisher?" Mary-Margaret asked.

Mr. Fisher walked over to the door and opened it.

"Why? Do either of you need a blood transfusion?" he said, motioning for his guests to leave. "Hardly any of your business. Now, if you don't mind."

They both got up and were almost out the door.

"Just one thing," Arthur said, turning back to face Mr. Fisher.

"Yes?" Mr. Fisher said, smirking.

"Where did you get that onyx brooch?"

He pointed to a black brooch sitting on the back of the stove.

"What?"

"That brooch. There," Arthur repeated, pointing it out.

"It was a gift."

"From who?" Arthur persisted.

"I don't think that's any of your business."

"And while we're at it, lad, what blood type are ye?" Mary-Margaret asked.

"I think you know more than you're letting on," Mr. Fisher said, moving past Arthur toward Mary-Margaret.

"I think you had better think twice before laying a hand on her," Arthur said, puffing out his chest.

"If that's a threat—"

"No, Mr. Fisher. It's a promise. From me," Arthur said, his dark glasses pulled down to the tip of his nose, his white cane held like an Escrima stick. "As well as being a master of disguises, I am also trained in the Filipino martial arts—"

"Look, I don't know what you two are up to—" Mr. Fisher started.

"I think you do," Arthur said, raising the white stick in the air as he stepped his right leg back, preparing to attack.

"Arthur, luv, I know ye mean well, but put the stick down," Mary-Margaret said before facing Mr. Fisher. "And it is ye who has some explainin' to do."

"And how do you figure that?" Mr. Fisher asked.

"Well, lad, ye have me friend's crucifix in yer house. No, not me friend's... me friend's daughter's crucifix. No mother would give anyone her daughter's crucifix, never mind take it off her own neck. And ye were too busy to attend her funeral, which is blasphemous, and now we have another lady's brooch sitting out plain as the day is long on top of yer stove. It doesn't add up, lad."

"You're both crazy, aren't you?" Mr. Fisher asked.

"Are we crazy, or are we onto somethin'?" Mary-Margaret asked.

"I'm good with crazy, but if you're that curious, perhaps you'd both like to sit back down," Mr. Fisher said, locking the door behind them as Mary-Margaret and Arthur resumed their places on the couch.

Chapter Thirty-Five

"I don't like the sound of this," Arthur whispered to Mary-Margaret..

"Stay steady," she whispered back.

"More water, anyone?" Mr. Fisher offered from the kitchen.

"I think we're all adequately hydrated, Mr. Fisher," Mary-Margaret replied. "If that's your real name."

"Suit yourselves. And yes, it is my real name. Why wouldn't it be? You must watch a lot of TV, Miss Marple."

"No, me son is a—"

"Anyone mind if I smoke?" Mr. Fisher asked.

"I've got asthma," Arthur said.

"Of course you do," Mr. Fisher replied with a broad smile, pulling a package of Gitanes from the top drawer beside the sink and putting one in his mouth. "But here, let me take your stick since you obviously don't need it."

Mr. Fisher casually walked over to Arthur, the unlit cigarette in his mouth, took the stick, and returned to the kitchen, putting the stick in the far corner of the room.

They sat in silence while he lit the cigarette on the stove burner, took a long inhale, and exhaled slowly, filling the air in front of him with a bluish smoke.

"So, how did I get the crucifix? No, wait. How did I get the brooch? Well..." He picked a strand of tobacco off his tongue. "Every time I buy a pack, I always vow I will only buy filtered the next time, and yet..."

He took another long drag. This time, he held it and then exhaled the smoke through his nose.

"Ye were sayin'," Mary-Margaret prompted.

"Right," Mr. Fisher said, coming around the kitchen island and then leaning against it to address his guests. "You could say that I'm a bit of a...ladies' man, as you've suggested, Miss Marple. And one of the things a ladies' man has to know is that not all ladies will like him."

"I think we'll be on our way now," Mary-Margaret said, starting to get up.

Mr. Fisher looked sharply at her. "I think you should stay. In fact, I've kind of warmed up to you. But not the hypochondriac."

"I am not a hypochondriac," Arthur objected. "All of my illnesses are well-documented."

"Enough," Mr. Fisher said, raising his voice.

"There are more of us than ye," Mary-Margaret pointed out, starting to sense that things might be going a bit contrary to her plan. "In case ye are thinkin' of—"

"I thought we were having a friendly chat. When did this get hostile? But, since you mention it," He stepped around the kitchen island and pulled a small revolver from the drawer. Mr. Fisher smiled, his voice soft again. "Let's all just take a deep breath and start again, shall we?"

"Well, this changes everythin', doesn't it?" Mary-Margaret said, her eyes fixed on the gun.

"I don't like the sound of this one bit," Arthur muttered to Mary-Margaret.

"We'll be alright, lad. Just give me a moment to think," Mary-Margaret whispered back.

"As I was saying, not every woman is going to like you when you're a ladies' man."

"Don't I know it," Arthur lamented.

"Stop talking," Mr. Fisher said, his voice rising again as he walked around the island to face them.

"Arthur, luv, I don't think this is the time," Mary-Margaret said softly.

"No, it's not. Listen to your grandmother, Arthur," Mr. Fisher warned, his voice hardening.

Mary-Margaret's back straightened as quickly as if she had been struck by lightning.

"So I had been dating a lovely lady," Mr. Fisher continued, his voice calm again as he leaned against the island, setting his gun down behind him, "from right here in the co-op. That's how I found out about this apartment. Put my name on the waitlist right away. They told me there weren't a lot of vacancies. Most people stay until the day they die."

"This wouldn't have been about six months ago, would it?" Mary-Margaret asked.

"A bit before that, but your timelines are about right," Mr. Fisher smiled. "But the guy who used to live here went into a nursing home. Nobody had to die for me to get in."

"Arthur, if ye have any nifty gizmos or gadgets, this would be the time—" Mary-Margaret whispered.

"Rolling," Arthur acknowledged, pushing his glasses back up on his face and staring directly at Mr. Fisher.

"I'm right here, people," Mr. Fisher said, waving his arms. "At least be discreet. Don't tell me you've got some sort of lapel camera going, sonny boy?"

"Hardly," Arthur chortled.

"Good. Now, as I was saying, things were going pretty well between me and my lady-friend, until they weren't. That's her onyx brooch, by the way. I gave it to her."

"And then she gave it back," Mary-Margaret said, nodding. "A love gone sour, no doubt."

"Something like that."

Arthur rubbed his chest. "Just a twinge. Nothing to worry about."

"Who said anyone was worried?" Mr. Fisher said, taking one last drag from the cigarette he had neglected, holding his right hand under it as the ash fell away.

"Left-handed, are we?" Mary-Margaret asked.

"Sign of genius, or so they say," Mr. Fisher smirked, turning to aggressively stub the cigarette out in the sink before turning back.

"So she gave the brooch back to ye, did she?" Mary-Margaret said.

"Yeah. She gave the brooch back. And that was that. And then—"

"Or did ye take it back?" Mary-Margaret asked.

"Does it matter? As you said, love gone sour."

"Only if she was still alive when ye took it back," Mary-Margaret replied. "Otherwise—"

"My, aren't we unhinged," Mr. Fisher said.

"Six months ago, another woman..." Mary-Margaret pressed.

"Curious, isn't it, that that was about the same time the woman I was dating broke it off with me," Mr. Fisher smiled condescendingly at her. "Don't you just love coincidences?"

"So how—" Arthur began.

"Don't rush me, Junior. I'm getting to that part."

He looked at the cigarette butt in the sink.

"You know, that was so good that I think I might have another one. Are you sure I can't offer you anything?" Mr. Fisher said, pulling another cigarette out of the package in the drawer. He stood back to observe his guests.

"About Jane Ann?" Mary-Margaret finally said.

"Right. Well, before we get into that, maybe I should answer a question you asked me before."

There was what seemed like a long pause before Mr. Fisher continued.

"A Positive."

"A positive what, luv?" Mary-Margaret asked, wanting to confirm what she already knew he meant.

There was a moment of silence.

"My blood type. A Positive. That's what you were looking for, wasn't it?"

"Tell me about Jane Ann Hill," Mary-Margaret said, her voice steady.

"She was a lovely woman. Seemed nice. Bright, warm, inquisitive, apparently had money at one point in her life. It was the money part that I most remember her for."

"How so?"

"She liked nice things. She told me she used to have a lot of them. Said she used to live in a place where she looked down on the whole city from her living room windows. By the time I met her, the whole city looked down on her. At least, that's how she felt."

"Doesn't sound like Jane Ann at all," Mary-Margaret objected.

"Well, I hate to burst your bubble, Granny, but that's how she felt. And that's kind of what did her in."

Mary-Margaret bristled at the word 'granny', but said simply, "I'm not followin'."

"Ninja Wannabe over here isn't the only person to notice the brooch. Which reminds me, I should be more careful in the future. And buy the filtered cigarettes." He picked another piece of tobacco off his tongue. "Jane Ann—lovely, bright, warm, greedy Jane Ann—noticed that onyx brooch as well. I was having some pangs of guilt about it at the time, so I told her the long version of how I ended up with her. It was kind of a painful story, so I made her promise to keep it between us."

"Well, if there's somethin' that woman could do, it was keepin' a secret."

"You must have known someone I didn't."

"Or you told her something she couldn't keep under her hat."

"I guess so, because she was going to tell the cops everything," Mr. Fisher said.

"What was there to tell?"

"Something that she thought was worth ten thousand dollars in cash."

"So she was goin' to blackmail ye?"

"Oh, it gets better," Mr. Fisher said, taking a drag from the cigarette. "I gave her ten grand. Cash. But she wanted another ten."

"That's a bit rich," Mary-Margaret admitted, praying that Arthur's video camera was working for what she hoped would turn into a full confession.

"Much richer than me," Mr. Fisher said with a dry laugh. "And so I killed her."

Mary-Margaret stopped breathing for a moment. And that's when she fully realized that she hadn't thought this situation through at all.

"Ye lost me there, lad," she said in an effort to buy herself that time to come up with a plan.

"Yeah. I went over to her place to get a cup of sugar—likely that same sugar I used for your booster juice, bucko, and she invited me in. Then, while she was getting it, she asked me if I had another ten grand to give her. I told her

I didn't, and as she was handing me the cup of sugar, that's when she told me that she would have no choice but to call the cops. So I killed her."

No one said a word for what seemed like a very long time.

"Well," Mary-Margaret finally said with a sigh but still no plan in place, "that's somethin', I suppose."

"Yeah. And now that I've told you and your friend, what am I going to do?"

Chapter Thirty-Six

"Don't look at me, lad," Mary-Margaret said. "I don't have a plan."

"Sounds like we're all in a bit of a bind, doesn't it?" Mr. Fisher said, a slight smile coming to his lips.

"Fear not, MM. I'm a trained—"

"Stop speaking," Mr. Fisher demanded.

"Best keep it to yerself, Arthur," Mary-Margaret said softly, taking her eyes off Mr. Fisher for a moment to nod quickly at Arthur.

"I think you should just let us go," Arthur said.

"Really? You think I should just let you go?" Mr. Fisher said, crossing his arms on his chest. "After I just told you that I killed Jane Ann? And we still haven't gotten to the part where I tell you how I got the onyx broach. Apparently, it's tied into some tragedy that coincides with this place and another unit becoming available at the same time. Imagine those odds. Maybe you should just sit tight for now."

"There are two of us and only one of you," Arthur said.

"I don't feel at all concerned," Mr. Fisher replied, looking dismissively at Arthur as he reached behind him for the gun.

"MM, think of something," Arthur whispered.

"I'm tryin', lad. I'm tryin'!"

"Well, then," Mr. Fisher said as he walked towards them, coming to an abrupt stop in the middle of the room. "Who wants to go first?"

"What do ye mean?" Mary-Margaret asked, her voice unsteady.

Mr. Fisher looked at the gun in his left hand and then looked back at Mary-Margaret and Arthur.

"Which one of you wants to lead us out that door, down the hallway, onto the street, and into my car? I know a lovely spot by the ravine."

"What is your emergency?" a woman's voice could be heard.

"What was that?" Mr. Fisher said, stepping back.

Mary-Margaret looked over at Arthur.

"What is your emergency?" the voice repeated.

"It's you, isn't it?" Mr. Fisher said, spitting out the words.

"If you are unable to answer, don't worry. I am just pulling up your file now, Mr.…. Pompanous, and I can see that you have a history of heart problems. I will be sending an ambulance to your location as soon as I get the GPS coordinates."

"Pompanous?" Mary-Margaret asked.

"I found it on the street when I was waiting for you," Arthur said, looking down at the medic alert necklace he was wearing. "Thought it might add to my disguise. I had no idea it was activated."

"I'm sorry. Did you say something, Mr. Pompanous?"

"Tell her you're fine. Tell her you're fine," Mr. Fisher hissed, pointing the gun at Arthur.

"I'm hearing more than one voice. Are you okay, Mr. Pompanous?"

"No, I'm not," Arthur said clearly.

"Don't worry, Mr. Pompanous. The ambulance is on its way. Just to confirm, you're at 25 Eden Street. Is that correct?"

"And ye had this all along and didn't think to use it give it a try until now?" Mary-Margaret asked.

"No!" Mr. Fisher yelled, pacing around the tiny apartment like a caged rat.

"Yes, that's correct," Arthur said to the dispatcher. "Total Hail Mary move, MM. I had no idea—"

"Now, I'm seeing that as a low-rise apartment building. What unit are you in, Mr. Pompanous?"

"104," Arthur said, and then added to Mary-Margaret, "I never go anywhere without knowing these things. I once was told that I—"

"I'm sorry, Mr. Pompanous. Are you alone or—?"

"No, I'm here with my friend Mary-Margaret and a man with a gun who wants to kill us."

"I'm sorry?"

"Yes. Please send the police."

"So you're telling me that you are someone with a gun who is wanting to harm—" the dispatcher began.

"The man with the gun has confessed to murderin' two women! And his name is...!" Mary-Margaret yelled into Arthur's chest.

"Shut. Up," Mr. Fisher screamed, rushing at Mary-Margaret with the gun.

"He may be killin' a third soon," Mary-Margaret shouted.

"Police are on the way, ma'am. Are you in immediate danger now?"

"I'd say so, yes," Mary-Margaret hollered, looking up at Mr. Fisher, who alternated between pointing the gun at Mary-Margaret and pacing the room.

"Are you able to get away to a place of safety?" the woman asked calmly.

"No. Oh, and tell the lads ye are sendin' that I'm Michael O'Shea's mam."

"Stop. Speaking!" Mr. Fisher yelled.

"I'm transferring this call over to the 9-1-1 operator now. Hello, 9-1-1?"

"'Tis Mary-Margaret O'Shea ye are on the line with," Mary-Margaret shouted. "We seem to have a bit of a situation here."

"Everyone! Stop!" Mr. Fisher shrieked, pointing the gun at Mary-Margaret.

"I understand there is a medical emergency and a murderer...?" came the voice of the 9-1-1 operator.

"Indeed, there is," Mary-Margaret replied.

Mr. Fisher bolted for the door. Arthur leapt up as Mr. Fisher fumbled to unlock it. Just as he got the door open, Arthur tackled Mr. Fisher to the ground.

"I'm a master of..." Arthur grunted while gasping for air, "a little-know battle art known as—"

"Get off of me," Mr. Fisher screamed, squirming and bucking, trying to get out from under Arthur, who was closer to triple than double his weight.

Arthur grabbed the gun from Mr. Fisher's hand and tossed it out into the hallway.

Mary-Margaret rushed to the kitchenette and grabbed Arthur's white hockey-stick-turned-cane from the far corner where Mr. Fisher had placed it. Then, just as Mr. Fisher appeared to be making some headway, she brought the stick out to her side and whacked Mr. Fisher with all of her might, knocking him out.

Arthur, soaked with sweat, got off of the motionless man. After adjusting his clothing, he pulled out a rope from inside his trench coat. He then rolled Mr. Fisher onto his side before tying his wrists and feet together behind his back.

"Recovery position is the safest under the circumstances," Arthur said, catching his breath while pushing his sticky hair off his forehead. "You were quite adept with that thing."

"And ye did yerself proud as well," Mary-Margaert said, catching her breath. "Is that the sirens I hear, then?"

Chapter Thirty-Seven

"Mom!" Michael yelled as he walked in through the open door, pushing past the paramedics.

"Michael. I knew ye would come," Mary-Margaret said, looking down over her shoulder from a stool in the kitchenette. "Arthur found one of those medical alarms, which is why the ambulance people are over there. And, what with all of the exertion, I need a cuppa. I don't suppose, bein' the Big City Detective that ye are, that you could deduce where our man here might be keepin' his tea?"

Michael looked around, trying to make some sense out of the scene in front of him. "I was out getting a coffee when I heard the call come over for this address. The dispatcher said something about a woman, saying she was a police officer's mother. I put two and two together and—"

"I always knew ye were bright, Michael. I don't know why they haven't named ye Police Officer of the Year yet. We can all live in hope, can't we?"

"Good job on the knots," one of the two uniformed officers who had followed quickly behind Michael told Arthur, placing the handcuffs on Mr. Fisher's wrists before undoing the ropes.

"Learned as a child. Always kind of fascinated me, really," Arthur said, holding his trench coat close to his body as he did up the buttons, concealing the secret stash of equipment that lined his coat to the officers.

"Got a full confession, did we," Mary-Margaret said, carefully stepping down from the stool, having given up on her hunt for tea.

"We'll need another car here to take each of them back to the station separately. Don't want them talking to one another before giving formal statements," Michael said to the first officer.

"No need for that. I've got the whole thing on video," Arthur said, pointing to his glasses.

"Sorry?" Michael said.

"Video. In the bridge here. I'll get it downloaded and email it to you—"

"Seize the glasses," Michael ordered the second officer.

Arthur raised a hand protectively towards his glasses as the young officer approached him.

"No need for any manhandlin', Michael," Mary-Margaret scolded. "I'm sure Arthur will—"

"This is a homicide investigation, Mom, not a—"

"Indeed. A homicide investigation I was able to…how do ye young ones say it?…bust wide open?"

Arthur gave her an enthusiastic thumb's up. "Yeah. That's about right, MM. I'd say you blew the top off of this one."

"That's a good thing, right?" Mary-Margaret said, smiling at Michael. "So while ye and yer lads are lookin' after our man, we'll all make our way to O'Leary's for—"

"No one is going anywhere," Michael said. "Except to the station. Call for another car. You can ride with me, Mom."

"I've me own car, Michael. I can drive meself," Mary-Margaret said.

"Why don't I believe you'll show up?"

"And I'll make my own way, thanks. I have a thing about riding in the back of police cars. Had a bad experience one time."

"No. I'll have a—"

"Ye'll do no such thing, Michael. And ye, Arthur, will hand the glasses over to Michael. There's the deal. Take it or leave it," Mary-Margaret stated.

The uniformed officers stared at Arthur and then at their detective, both of whom were staring at Mary-Margaret.

"Take it," she said slowly, "or leave it." "Suit yourself," Michael finally said. "Just make sure you show up. And give me those glasses."

Michael held out his hand, and Arthur reluctantly handed the glasses over to him.

Chapter Thirty-Eight

"Well, are ye puttin' the kettle on, or am I?" Mary-Margaret said as she and Michael walked through the back door of the house. Phil came charging at them.

"Ach, wee Phil. Likely about to burst at the seams. Take the pup out for a piddle." Mary-Margaret handed Michael the dog's leash from the back of the door along with a couple of stoop-and-scoop bags. "Just in case, ye know. And before ye go, turn the burner on while I go to the jacks meself."

Micheal grimaced as he clipped the leash on the dog and let them both out the door he had just walked through.

"Ta, luv," Mary-Margaret said as she came back downstairs, dropping into one of the chairs before reaching for her mug of tea. "This is wonderful. Nothin' like a cuppa after a day such as this to make everythin' better. Am I right, or am I right?"

She took a long sip from the mug.

Just then, there was a knock on the front door. Michael got up to answer it.

"Oh, I'm sorry," a familiar voice began. "I must have the wrong house. Or are you Mary-Margaret's son?"

"Oh, for the love of...." Mary-Margaret muttered.

"Yes, I am. And she's here. Mom?" Michael said over his shoulder. "Someone here to see you."

Laura-Jean McQueen stepped inside as Mary-Margaret came to the door.

"I'm so sorry to bother you at your son's home like this, Mary-Margaret, but I have a confession to make."

"Then yer in the wrong house," Mary-Margaret snapped.

"Would you like to come in and sit down?" Michael offered.

Mary-Margaret glared at him.

"No. I'm fine. Thank you." Laura-Jean took a deep breath. "Mary-Margaret, I-I-I almost...it was me who almost ran you off the road after the bazaar."

"What?" Mary-Margaret said.

"It was an accident," Laura-Jean began. "I was pretty put out when I left that day, but that's not what caused me to—"

"That's fine, luv," Mary-Margaret said, taking the woman by the shoulders to lead her out of the entryway. "No need to explain. Ye see, Michael? 'Twas not a lunati...well, 'twas Laura-Jean."

"Maybe you'd better come in and sit down," Michael repeated.

"No. I'm sure she's fine. I accept yer apology, Laura-Jean. Safe travels," Mary-Margaert said, closing the door as soon as Laura Jean was on the front stoop.

"What was that all about?" Michael said as they returned to their seats.

"Ach, it matters not," she said, looking at her tea. "Perhaps, after the day we've had, we'd be better off with a wee dram."

Phil's whole body wagged as Michael poured them both a healthy shot from the bottle of fine whiskey he kept on hand for such occasions.

Just as Michael was handing the glass to Mary-Margaret, there was a knock at the back door.

"Ach. 'Tis like Grand Central Station around here," Mary-Margaret said.

"Come on in, Arthur," Michael said as Arthur was letting himself in with his cleaner's key. "Here. Have a drink. I'll pour myself another."

"MM," Arthur said as he took the glass and pushed past Michael to sit in the chair beside her.

"What? No costume? I must say, lad, I'm a bit disappointed," Mary-Margaret said with a smile.

"I'm just glad to be out of that police station. I thought they'd never be done."

"Are ye just finishin' up now, luv? Michael, why would it take them so long—"

"Not my case," Michael said with a sigh. Standing back, raising his newly-filled glass. "Here's to us and everyone wishing they were!"

The three raised their glasses.

"Sláinte."

Acknowledgements

Thank you, Cindy Bullard (Birch Literary), for seeing the magic in Mary-Margaret.

About the Author

Desmond P. Ryan was born and raised in Toronto, Canada. He completed an honors Bachelor of Arts Degree in English Literature and Political Science at the University of Toronto before spending the next thirty years as a detective with the Toronto Police Service.

He now resides in a neighborhood in Toronto known as Cabbagetown, where he spends his time writing, teaching, and wandering off to the pub.

SOCIAL MEDIA HANDLES:
@RealDesmondRyan (Twitter)
DesmondPRyan (Insta)
Desmond P Ryan (YouTube)

AUTHOR WEBSITE:
RealDesmondRyan.com

Also by Desmond P. Ryan

10-33 Assist PC, The Mike O'Shea Series, book 1, Level Best Books

Death Before Coffee, The Mike O'Shea Series, book 2, Level Best Books

Man at the Door, The Mike O'Shea Series, book 3, Level Best Books

"Cold Comfort." *To Serve, Protect, and Write: Cops Writing Crime Fiction, vol. 1,* A.B. Patterson, Broadway, NSW, 2022.